Bolan leaped from the Niva carrying the RPG-7.

Behind him, he heard Sabah Azmeh jump out and make a run for it, as instructed. Not that it would help, if the advancing chopper's searchlight fell on either one of them.

Whether it was a Hind  er, neither could shru an's 93 mm roc e could bring down t to be—if he h

He'd have to rst time. He hadn't grabbed a second rocket from the Niva's backseat, and he likely wouldn't have time to reload the launcher anyway, if his first warhead missed its mark.

The searchlight found his ride, swept to the pilot's right and froze on Bolan.

He recognized the stutter of a heavy machine gun and saw its muzzle flashes winking at him from the helicopter's chin. That meant he had a Hind to deal with and would have to make a clean hit with his HEAT round when he let it fly.

First, though, Bolan had to dodge the storm of bullets streaming toward him. He hit the ground and rolled, took a beating on his shoulder from the launcher's tube, and came up in a crouch, squinting through its sight into the searchlight's blinding glare.

MACK BOLAN ®
The Executioner

THE EXECUTIONER®

DON PENDLETON'S

SYRIAN RESCUE

A GOLD EAGLE BOOK FROM
W✷RLDWIDE®

TORONTO • NEW YORK • LONDON
AMSTERDAM • PARIS • SYDNEY • HAMBURG
STOCKHOLM • ATHENS • TOKYO • MILAN
MADRID • WARSAW • BUDAPEST • AUCKLAND

For Staff Sergeant Melvin Morris

First edition September 2015

ISBN-13: 978-0-373-64442-1

Special thanks and acknowledgment to
Mike Newton for his contribution to this work.

Syrian Rescue

Recycling programs
for this product may
not exist in your area.

Civil war? What does that mean? Is there any foreign war? Is not every war between men, war between brothers?

—Victor Hugo, *Les Misérables*

Borders will not keep me from hunting down those who kill their brothers and sisters for personal gain. Willing or not, those criminals are at war with The Executioner.

—Mack Bolan

THE
MACK BOLAN
LEGEND

Nothing less than a war could have fashioned the destiny of the man called Mack Bolan. Bolan earned the Executioner title in the jungle hell of Vietnam.

But this soldier also wore another name—Sergeant Mercy. He was so tagged because of the compassion he showed to wounded comrades-in-arms and Vietnamese civilians.

Mack Bolan's second tour of duty ended prematurely when he was given emergency leave to return home and bury his family, victims of the Mob. Then he declared a one-man war against the Mafia.

He confronted the Families head-on from coast to coast, and soon a hope of victory began to appear. But Bolan had broken society's every rule. That same society started gunning for this elusive warrior—to no avail.

So Bolan was offered amnesty to work within the system against terrorism. This time, as an employee of Uncle Sam, Bolan became Colonel John Phoenix. With a command center at Stony Man Farm in Virginia, he and his new allies—Able Team and Phoenix Force—waged relentless war on a new adversary: the KGB.

But when his one true love, April Rose, died at the hands of the Soviet terror machine, Bolan severed all ties with Establishment authority.

Now, after a lengthy lone-wolf struggle and much soul-searching, the Executioner has agreed to enter an "arm's-length" alliance with his government once more, reserving the right to pursue personal missions in his Everlasting War.

Prologue

Deir ez-Zor Governorate, Syria

Yaser Jenyat was sick of waiting. It was miserably hot and the dry earth underneath his buttocks was scorching. When he checked his Rolex replica, it seemed the hands were frozen. Had they moved at all since he had checked them last?

"They've changed plans, or itineraries," he suggested. "Maybe someone warned them."

"Who?" Ziad Dalila asked him.

"How should I know?" Jenyat answered. "Someone."

"We have orders," said Malek Hakim.

"We have obeyed them," Jenyat shot back. "We came, we waited. No one said we have to take up residence."

"You want to leave," Hakim replied, "start walking."

Jenyat tried to spit but found his mouth had suddenly gone dry. "I didn't say that." His voice cracked like the sunbaked soil. "We *all* should go, before a damned patrol turns up."

"You know these Westerners," Tawfiq Jandali said. "They're slow with everything."

Until they want to kill you, Jenyat thought. Shifting where he sat, his back against the left rear tire of their UAZ-469 off-road vehicle, his elbow grazed the AKM assault rifle standing beside him, almost toppling it before he lunged and caught it, just in time. He glanced around to see if any of the others had observed his clumsiness, but they were busy squinting at the eastern skyline, toward Iraq.

"We'll wait another thirty minutes," Hakim said. "If they're not here by then, I'll call in for advice."

No one replied to that. It had not been a question.

Jenyat sipped warm water out of his canteen. He wished they had some shade, that someone else had drawn the so-called "plum assignment," that he might be anyplace but here. The thoughts of glory he'd envisioned when his name was drawn had long since disappeared, evaporating like the sweat that drenched his shirt.

At least he would not be the one to fire the crucial shot. He understood the basics of the 9K338 Igla-S shoulder-mounted launcher and its 9M342 missile, but he was not competent to aim and fire it, thank Allah. If they had waited all this time only to fail at their assignment, Jenyat was relieved the shame would not be his.

"I see something," Dalila said, passing Hakim his field glasses. "East-northeast."

That covered half the godforsaken desert, but Hakim had barely raised the glasses to his eyes when he said, "I see it." Several seconds later he added, "Yes. It's them."

Jenyat rose to his feet, surprised to feel a fleeting tremor in his legs, and reached for his rifle. He would have no use for it, if all went well, but he felt better holding it, sharing the AKM's potential for explosive violence.

"Get ready," Hakim ordered.

Tawfiq was even now hauling the Igla out of the UAZ-469's cargo bay. The tube was painted olive drab, like everything else in the army. It was a little over five feet long, nose-heavy with its pistol grip and its bulbous infrared sighting gear. Already loaded, it weighed thirty-seven pounds, including the warheads. Its maximum operational range was almost four miles, with a flight ceiling of eleven and a half thousand feet.

They had been promised that the target, although capable of cruising at much higher altitudes, would be within the missile's range. The flight would be a border hop, evading radar on both sides to keep the visit under wraps. Deniability was crucial to diplomacy among the states that labeled themselves civilized.

"Late as they are, how do we know it's them?" he asked Hakim.

"I see the plane," Hakim replied. "It has 'UN' painted behind the cockpit and on the tail."

"Praise Allah," Ziad Dalila said.

"Allahu akbar," Jandali chimed in, as he hoisted the launcher to his right shoulder.

Jenyat could see the target now, and he heard the whisper of its twin engines drawing closer. He considered praying briefly, silently, but then decided it would be a waste of time.

Squinting, he watched the small white speck, distorted by the heat haze, moving into range.

"I WILL REMIND you that we must not set our hopes too high," Sani Bankole said.

Seated across the aisle from Bankole, Roger Segrest almost asked, "what hopes?" but stopped himself. He was a pessimist by nature but had learned to hide it well during his long climb up the State Department ladder to his present post. Most of the people he dealt with daily lived for smiles and reassurances, not straight talk that would drive them all to drink.

Besides, he didn't have to spell it out. Segrest was confident that everyone aboard the Let L 410 was wise enough to know the truth—namely, that Syria was in the toilet, circling the drain. The country had been bad enough, a nest of terrorists, before its latest civil war erupted, pitting a despotic government against hundreds of rival "liberation" forces. Toss in Hezbollah, the Kurds and ISIS, among other players, and what did you have?

A goddamned recipe for disaster.

Still, there was an outside chance he and the other passengers on this plane might accomplish *something*, he supposed. Stranger things had happened in the strange world of diplomacy, but they were few and far between.

One of the pilots spoke up on the intercom. "We've crossed the border, gentlemen."

Segrest couldn't have told the difference, peering out his window at the trackless wasteland below. All deserts looked the same to him: bleak, unforgiving, dangerous.

He idly wondered what their lodgings would be like in Deir ez-Zor. They'd be stuck in the Syrian city for three or four days, unless the talks broke down immediately—as they might, considering the endless grievances both sides advanced.

Make that all sides, Segrest thought. It might have been a relatively simple matter if the only people at the table had been government officials and the rebels who opposed them. Oil, politics and religion changed that, of course, dragging in Lebanon, Iraq, Israel and Jordan, not to mention Russia and his own employer, the United States. They hadn't heard from China yet, or Egypt, but he wouldn't be surprised if both of them weighed in before the year was out.

Diplomacy, my ass, he thought, only half listening to their putative spokesman from the United Nations. It was a damned chess game, with better than a dozen players making moves.

"But if we have patience—" Bankole was on a roll, but now the cockpit intercom cut through his platitudes.

"We have a target lock! Fasten your seat belts, gentlemen. Evasive action, starting now!"

Segrest looked out the window, didn't see a damned thing but the pale blue sky they occupied and the broiling desert. "Target lock" meant someone had "painted" them with infrared to guide a rocket or a burst of anti-aircraft fire, but who in the hell—

The Let L 410 shuddered, riding a blast of thunder from the clear sky. The explosion didn't breach the cabin, but oxygen masks automatically dropped from the ceiling, dangling like weird wilted flowers in front of their faces. Segrest fumbled with his seat belt, fastening it on the third try, as the turboprop nosed over and began to fall.

Even the pilot sounded panicked. "Crash positions, gentlemen! We're going down."

1

Deir ez-Zor Governorate, Syria

The Jeep Wrangler was twenty-plus years old and showed it, mangy rust spots peeking through its faded paint, a long crack stretching across the lower left-hand quadrant of its dusty windshield. The canvas roof rattled and flapped. Its seats were sprung, their stuffing visible where seams had split, and underneath a set of worn-out rubber mats, passengers could watch the desert rolling past below, if they were so inclined.

Mack Bolan didn't care about the Jeep's appearance or its comfort. Before accepting it, he'd checked the tires—not new by any means, but serviceable—and the 4.2-liter engine, testing out the four-wheel drive, until he was more or less convinced that it would take him where he had to go and bring him back again.

Maybe.

A lot of that depended on terrain, of course, and any

obstacles—human or otherwise—they met along the way. So far, they had been making fairly decent time.

The man riding in the shotgun seat was a slender Syrian with a patchy beard, wearing a checkered *keffiyeh* and faded desert camouflage, the sleeves rolled up, pants cuffs tucked into well-worn combat boots. He had a pistol and a wicked dagger in the waistband of his trousers, hidden by the loose tail of his four-pocket BDU shirt.

The heavy hardware rode behind them, on the Wrangler's floorboard and backseat.

They had left Highway 7 ten miles north of Al Mayadin, angling northeastward on a road that wasn't marked on any map, barely a shadow of a line on Google Earth. No one had ever bothered paving it or even laying gravel down. Why waste the time and energy, when desert winds and shifting sand could cover and conceal it within minutes?

"We are in bandit country now," Sabah Azmeh observed.

"I'm more concerned about the army and irregulars," Bolan replied.

"They're bandits, too. They just have newer clothes and weapons."

That was true enough. Deir ez-Zor Governorate harbored armed forces of various factions in Syria's long civil war. Bolan was hoping to avoid them all and complete his mission with a minimum of static, but he knew that notion wasn't realistic; hence, the hardware in the back.

Beyond armed opposition, there was still the desert to contend with—over ten thousand square miles of nothing but sand, stone, scorpions and cobras. Water was scarce, cover likewise, and the only ally he had was riding in the Wrangler's shotgun seat.

Azmeh spat out a curse and pointed off to Bolan's left, toward a plume of beige dust rising in the still, hot air. One vehicle, at least, and it was headed their way. "If they're hostile, we'll deal with it," said Bolan. "Grab the rifles."

Azmeh twisted in his seat and rummaged underneath a tatty blanket covering a portion of their mobile arsenal. He fished out two AKMS assault rifles, their metal stocks folded, both with forty-round box magazines in place, loaded with 7.62×39 mm rounds.

"It's too bad," Azmeh said.

"Too bad," Bolan agreed.

But the encounter was unavoidable.

"YOU SEE IT?" Youssef Sadek asked his driver.

"It's hard to miss," Sami Karam replied.

"Get after them."

Karam changed course to chase the distant rooster tail of dust, downshifting first, then bringing the GAZ Sadko cargo truck up to speed. Their men in the back would be cursing by now, maybe craning their necks for a glimpse of whatever had drawn them off course.

Karam knew the drill: stop and search anyone they found drifting around in the desert, unless they were Syrian regulars. Karam and his men were Hezbollah fighters, and their party had long sided with the Syrian government.

"One vehicle, I think," Sadek observed, talking to help himself relax. It was a trait Karam had noticed in the past but did not share.

"Perhaps one," he replied, to keep from being rude.

"Not large," Sadek said. "Maybe a UAZ."

"Maybe," Karam agreed, scanning the desert that still lay between them and their quarry.

"You can overtake them, eh?"

"I hope so."

The GAZ Sadko had a 4.67-liter V8 engine, generating 130 horsepower, but the truck could only do so much off-road, on rough terrain, without falling apart or pitching the soldiers out of its open bed like popcorn bursting from a pot with no lid.

Karam fought the steering wheel and grappled with the gearshift, sharp eyes twitching from his target—which was definitely fleeing now—to the ground in front of him, watching out for hidden obstacles. The last thing he needed was to crash against a boulder or tip into a wadi that he'd overlooked.

The one thing worse than meeting unexpected adversaries in the desert would be getting stranded there, long miles from any help. The Sadko had no radio, of course, and while Karam was carrying a cell phone, picking up a signal here would be impossible.

So, no mistakes, then.

"Faster!" Sadek urged him, as if simply saying it would make the truck perform beyond its capabilities.

Karam said nothing, concentrating on the smaller vehicle ahead of them. The gap was closing, though not fast enough to please his agitated passenger. Sadek enjoyed killing—well, who didn't?—but he sometimes rushed into a fight without considering the possibility of failure.

Closer now, Karam could see that they were following an ancient Jeep, not an official army vehicle. That still left many possibilities, given the Governorate's state of near chaos. For all Karam knew, they might even now be wasting time and fuel, chasing a party of their so-called friends: the Badr Corps or the Promised Day Brigade—they were too numerous to count on any given day.

Focus on what you know, he thought.

Four passengers at most inside the Jeep, which meant they were outnumbered more than two to one by Karam and his men. Fair odds, but you could never truly judge an enemy until you joined him in battle.

And if you had misjudged him…

Karam had to be prepared when they made contact. Wedged between his left knee and the driver's door, his AK-47 was already locked and loaded. He could bail out of the truck, firing, or run down anyone who tried to flee the Jeep on foot.

Beyond that, all Karam could do was clutch the steering wheel and pray.

"They're gaining on us," Azmeh said.

Bolan could see that in his rearview, and he didn't care to comment on the obvious. Instead, he asked, "So, any thoughts on who they are?"

"The truck is standard issue," Azmeh said. "But no flag or insignia. Not army or police, then, but beyond that—anyone."

That helped a little. Bolan drew a private line at killing cops, regardless of what side they served or how corrupt they were.

The problem now: assuming that he couldn't lose the truck pursuing them, where could they stand and fight?

The flat, featureless desert offered no concealment, nothing in the way of cover if he stopped to shoot it

out. Bolan could see heads bobbing in the truck's bed,
men with rifles who would likely have no qualms about
eliminating him. At the moment, Bolan didn't know
who was pursuing them. They might be Syrians or Leb-
anese, Jordanians or Kurds, Iraqis or Iranians, Sunnis
or Shi'ites.

And it made no difference. He had to take them out.

The hardware Bolan had on hand was standard issue,
for convenience. His pistol, like Azmeh's, was the same
Browning Hi-Power carried by Syrian army officers.
The other arms were Russian, from their matched
AKMs to a Dragunov SVD sniper rifle, an RPK light
machine gun, an RPG-7 grenade launcher with a mix
of warheads, and a case of F1 hand grenades known in
the Motherland as *limonka* for their supposed resem-
blance to lemons.

First thing, Bolan scratched the long-range weapons
off his mental list. His Dragunov was loaded, packing
ten rounds in a detachable box magazine, but the rifle
was meant for solitary, unsuspecting targets at a distance. He could use it to stop the truck, sure, if he took
the driver out or maybe cracked the engine block, but
would leave shooters scampering around the desert,
no fit job for the Dragunov's PSO-1 telescopic sight.

It would be down and dirty, then, a bloody scramble with their vehicles as the only cover, in a firefight
where the Jeep was nearly as important as their own
flesh and blood. If they lost their transportation, their
mission was a washout.

Trapped in Syria on foot, they were as good as dead.

Bolan checked the Jeep's fuel gauge: three-quarters
full, two hundred fifty miles or so before the tank would
run dry. They had spare cans of gasoline in back, but

those were vulnerable to incoming fire, the first thing that a random burst might ventilate. Besides, he couldn't hope to ditch the truck simply by outpacing it. For starters, it would have a larger gas tank—maybe two, three times the size of the Jeep's—and even with its greater weight it could outlast the Wrangler in the long run.

No, they'd have to fight. The only questions now were when and where.

"Be ready when I give the word," he warned Azmeh. "Don't hesitate."

"I will not."

Bolan stood on the accelerator, racing over rocky ground that sent jolts through his spine, still looking for a place to make a stand.

"WHY ARE YOU slowing down?" Sadek demanded.

"I'm trying not to wreck the truck," Karam replied, tight-lipped.

"We cannot let them get away!" Sadek spat back at him.

Karam had no answer for that, but Sadek felt the truck accelerate a little in response to his tirade. A little, yes, but not enough to suit him.

They had spent the past two days patrolling empty landscapes, wasting time and fuel. Returning to his captain empty-handed made Sadek feel like a fool. It marked him, he was sure, as someone who could not perform to expectations. Someone who should not advance to a higher rank. He hated feeling like a failure, even though the purpose of jihad was serving Allah, not one's self. Another flaw in Sadek's character, but one he'd learned to live with over time.

He turned to peer at his men through the cab's rear

window. They were rocking with the truck, clinging to their weapons and their bench seats. Some, the younger ones, were smiling, happy to be hunting, while the more experienced among them were expressionless. The veterans had been through this before, with variations: travelers detained and questioned, then released if they identified themselves as allies, executed if they failed to prove their allegiance. Each enemy eliminated was another victory, however insignificant it seemed.

And this quarry was running. That proved something to Sadek.

He would not allow them to escape.

"Enough of this," he snarled, lifting his AK-47 from between his knees. He twisted in his seat and eased the rifle through his open window, sling around his right arm to prevent it from falling if his sweaty hands slipped.

"Youssef..." Karam warned.

"We have to stop them," Sadek said as he tried to aim, a rush of hot air in his face, making him squint.

His first short burst was wasted, rattling off to the far right of the fleeing Jeep. Cursing, Sadek tried to correct his aim, but it was difficult, the door's sun-heated metal nearly blistering his bare arms while the jolting of the truck made the Kalashnikov's adjustable iron sights vibrate erratically.

He fired again, four rounds on full-auto, and imagined that he saw one punch a divot in the old Jeep's fender. An improvement, but he had to do better if he meant to stop them.

Another rifle fired somewhere above him, making Sadek flinch. One of his men had followed his example, shooting at the Jeep. A flash of irritation stung him, then he realized it did not matter who managed to stop the vehicle, as long as it was done. A second rifle rattling overhead made Sadek smile.

The travelers had doomed themselves by running, even if they were not enemies. His men were hunting, and they wanted blood. So did Sadek, if he was honest with himself.

Now, if Karam would only hold the truck steady enough for him to aim…

A BULLET STRUCK the Wrangler's right wing mirror, ripping it away. Sabah Azmeh slumped lower in his seat, half turned to watch the truck behind them slowly gaining ground. Two riflemen were aiming across the truck cab's roof, a third man leaning from the passenger's window, rifle in hand.

How had he come to this?

The answer mocked him: he had volunteered.

"I'll try to slow them down," Azmeh told the tall American who called himself Matt Cooper.

"Good luck," Cooper replied, seeming to mean it.

Given how much they were swerving to avoid incoming fire, Azmeh couldn't crawl into the rear. The best he could do was aim his AKMS through the hazy back window, hold steady when he fired, and hope the hot brass spewing from his weapon did not fall down Cooper's collar, burning him and maybe causing him to crash the Jeep.

Azmeh braced one elbow on the low back of his seat to help steady his weapon, which was switched to semiautomatic. He didn't think he could stop the truck, much less take out its occupants, but if he slowed them down a bit, perhaps Cooper could think of something.

Azmeh's first shot drilled through the window's yel-
lowed plastic and flew on, hopefully to strike the truck.
Azmeh would have loved to drill its radiator, stranding
their assailants and leaving them to simmer through the
afternoon and freeze overnight.

That mental picture cheered him, and he fired twice
more before an enemy bullet pierced the Jeep's window.
Azmeh flinched and ducked as it struck the roll bar and
shattered, spraying the seats with shrapnel. Something
stung his left arm.

"Full-auto now, I think," he said to Cooper.

"Your call," the American replied, and somehow
found a way to wring more speed out of the Wrangler's howling engine.

AT LEAST THREE RIFLEMEN were firing at them now, by
Bolan's count. He couldn't see them well, between the
dust, his wobbling mirrors and the Wrangler's canvas
top, but they were gaining, and their prospects for a hit
seemed better than Azmeh's. Bolan was locked out of
the action, doing what he could to dodge incoming fire
without rolling the Jeep. He hoped there were no wadis
hiding out there, waiting to derail them in the next few
hundred yards.

Azmeh squeezed off another burst, then muttered
something to himself. Before Azmeh fired again, Bolan
called out, raising his voice over the wind. "I want to
try something. Fasten your seat belt."

Azmeh didn't question him. He had to know that
they were running out of time and options now. If Bolan
couldn't pull off a surprise for their pursuers, they were
toast.

He heard the seat belt click and said, "Okay, hang on!"

Cranking the Wrangler's wheel hard to the left, he whipped the Jeep's rear end through a long, sliding one hundred eighty-degree turnaround. The knobby tires spewed sand and gravel, raising clouds of dust.

Before it settled, Bolan scooped up his Kalashnikov and bailed out of the Jeep, leaving Azmeh to follow him as they went to meet their enemies.

Whatever happened next would be on Bolan's terms.

2

Washington, DC

"How much do you know about the Syrian civil war?" Hal Brognola had asked Bolan, thirty-odd hours earlier.

"The basics," Bolan had replied. "The president's been hanging on for what, twelve years?"

"Fourteen and counting," Brognola replied.

"He came up through the army, he's a critic of the West, not much regard for human rights. The Arab Spring surprised him, like it did other leaders in the region. Where they folded, he's clung to power, with accusations of atrocities against the rebels and civilians. He's got the army and police, supported by Iran and outside Shi'ite groups. The opposition is a shaky coalition—Kurds, the Muslim Brotherhood, Sufis opposed to Shi'ites, take your pick."

Brognola nodded. "So, you know the diplomatic picture, more or less."

"Broad strokes," Bolan said.

"Okay, well you won't have heard about the new initiative. It's strictly classified—which, given the UN's Swiss cheese security, means only ten or fifteen thousand people know about it. Long story short, a couple of people from State have been talking to Syrian opposition leaders and an undersecretary from UNESCWA. In case that doesn't ring a bell, it's the United Nations Economic and Social Commission for Western Asia, concerned with all things Middle Eastern."

"Talking? That's the secret?"

"Nope. The secret bit is *where* they were supposed to hold their latest talks. In Syria, at Ar-Raqqah, east of the capital. They planned to slip in from Iraq, under the radar, have their sit-down, offer the rebels whatever they need to get rid of the president and restore civil order."

"Not the UN's usual approach."

"Not even close," Hal said. "And that's why it was on the QT, more or less."

"When you say 'was'…"

"They tried it, yesterday, but something happened. No one's sure exactly what that was. We've lost track of the UN flight from Baghdad—radio silence, no SOS to indicate that they were going down."

"What about the beacons?"

"There were two on board, as usual," Brognola said. "A distress radio beacon and an underwater locator retrofitted to the standard flight recorder. So far, neither one of them is functioning."

"That seems unusual."

"Extremely," Brognola agreed. "One of the guys from State was also wearing an emergency locator transmitter, but he would have had to turn it on himself. So far, nothing. Could be it slipped his mind, or maybe he's no longer with us."

Bolan saw where this was going. "And you need someone to take a look," he said, not asking.

"Right."

"What have you got from satellite surveillance, so far?"

"Squat. Before we knew the plane was missing, a haboob blew in from the Sahara, dumping tons of sand all along the projected flight path. If the plane went down, it's hidden from us now."

"That isn't much to go on," Bolan said.

"Not much, but we need to try. Aside from our guys and the UN delegates, there were people from the opposition on the plane. They've been to Washington, been seen around the White House. If the Syrian army or their playmates bag the drop-ins, it's a black eye for the States and the United Nations. Makes it look like we were setting up an end run to resolve the civil war."

"We were," Bolan observed.

"Which doesn't mean the world's supposed to know it," Brognola reminded him.

Deniability. One of the oldest games in politics, diplomacy and war.

"Anything else I should know?" asked Bolan.

"Other than the fact that time is of the essence?" Brognola removed a flash drive from an inside pocket of his jacket, handing it to Bolan. "Files on the missing personnel. Same password as usual."

Bolan nodded and pocketed the device.

"So, as I said, time's critical, and we're already behind the game. You have a seven-thirty reservation from Dulles out to London Heathrow, where we have a seat waiting on a flight to Baghdad. You'll be met there, with arrangements for the crossing into Syria."

"Equipment?"

"Waiting for you at the other end. Top quality. Deniable, of course."

"Of course. Special instructions?"

"There's a chance you'll be too late. I'd call it fifty-fifty, given all that's going on in eastern Syria. In which case—"

"It's a rescue mission," Bolan finished for him.

Brognola nodded grimly. "That's the best case scenario."

ONCE HE'D CHECKED IN and cleared security at Dulles, Bolan found a seat at his gate and opened his laptop to review the files on the USB key.

There wasn't that much to them. But running down the list gave Bolan a feel for those who had been aboard the UN flight, matching names to photographs and fleshing out the details of their lives.

The head honcho on the flight was Sani Bankole, forty-seven-year-old from Nigeria. He had joined the Ministry of Foreign Affairs at twenty-one and worked his way up from there to his current UN post as deputy undersecretary-general for UNESCWA. His rank carried diplomatic immunity, which, Bolan thought, would mean precisely nothing in the devil's mix of Syria.

Bankole's number two was Tareq Eleyan, a thirty-six-year-old Jordanian. Most likely, he had been assigned to translate and to offer insight on the mind-set of his country's neighbors to the north. Roger Segrest led the US team. Age fifty-two, he was one of four deputy secretaries from the State Department's Executive

Secretariat. That job normally involved liaison between State and the White House or the National Security Council, but it seemed Segrest was branching out. His backup, barely half Segrest's age, was Dale Walton, a relative fledgling with eight years at State. He had a master's from Columbia in Middle Eastern history and politics, and he was fluent in Arabic. Beyond that, there was nothing else of interest in Walton's dossier.

The mission's wild cards came from Syria. Muhammad Qabbani was an old-looking forty, highly placed in the National Coalition for Syrian Revolutionary and Opposition Forces. That group, as Bolan knew, was constantly in flux, but Qabbani managed a delicate tightrope act within it, working to alleviate dissension in the ranks, mediating personality clashes between spokesmen for such disparate partners as the Muslim Brotherhood, the Kurdish National Council and the al-Nusra Front, affiliated with al-Qaeda. Qabbani's second was Rafic Al Din. He'd been imprisoned by the regime for joining demonstrations in the Arab Spring, then caught a break when amnesty was briefly offered in a bid to pacify the West. He'd joined the Free Syrian Army, and the rest of his file was a blank, presumably involving covert work that wasn't on the record.

Bolan didn't care for wild cards, but he'd worked with many in the past—sometimes successfully, sometimes not so much. His present mission, if he found the diplomats at all, would not allow him time to argue or cajole the targets into playing ball with him, accepting orders from a man they'd never met before and never would again. He'd have to pull rank, seize control—a problem in itself.

Bolan's experience with other members of the diplomatic breed enabled him to profile these men with fair precision. Even in this extremity, they'd be suspicious of outsiders turning up out of the blue and giving orders. There could be resistance, possibly defiance from the men he'd been assigned to save.

Closing the laptop, Bolan made a private resolution not to fail.

It was a do-or-die assignment. Fifty-fifty. Right.

Baghdad International Airport

THE AIRPORT'S SINGLE terminal was crowded as Bolan deplaned, shouldering his carry-on. Greeters were lined up with signs on the far side of passport control, and Bolan recognized his contact from Brognola's flash drive. Sabah Azmeh was holding a piece of white cardboard with "COOPER" written across it.

"That's me," Bolan said, as he approached the smaller man. Azmeh wore a blue blazer over khakis and well-worn loafers.

"Mr. Cooper, excellent!" He beamed, but there were still formalities to be observed. "A journey of a thousand miles begins with but a single step," he added.

"Not all who wander are lost," Bolan replied, completing the exchange.

"Indeed." Still smiling, Azmeh pumped his hand three times, then let it go. His grip was strong and dry. "Do you have other luggage?"

"Just this," Bolan answered, hoisting his lone bag.

"Perfect. A man who travels light, yes? We'll find our vehicle outside and then perhaps collect some heavy baggage."

They headed out to the parking lot and got into the

Wrangler. Once they were on the move, with Azmeh driving, Bolan asked him, "Was there any problem with the hardware?"

"No, no. Nothing whatsoever. Weapons and explosives are as common in Baghdad today as vegetables. Perhaps more so."

Bad news for residents whose only goal was to get on with normal life, but good for Bolan when he'd traveled halfway round the world unarmed. He'd grown accustomed to flying unarmed, but working the streets of a city like Baghdad without hardware made him feel naked.

On their way to meet the weapons' dealer, Bolan filled out Azmeh's sketchy dossier from Stony Man. His guide was twenty-eight, a Syrian expatriate who'd lost his parents and three younger siblings to a chemical attack at Ghouta in August 2013. Prior to that, the Syrian police had killed his older brother, leaving Azmeh as the sole survivor of his family. Despite those losses, he seemed fairly cheerful—or he'd learned to fake it. Instead of joining rebel forces to unseat the regime, Azmeh still hoped his homeland might achieve stability without more slaughter. To that end, he'd signed on as a native asset of the CIA and volunteered for Bolan's mission when it came around.

Bolan was cautious, hoped that Azmeh wasn't lying to him, and that no one from the Company was playing games behind the scenes, pursuing some agenda they had kept from Brognola. When they'd stocked up on hardware, clothing for the field, and everything they needed to survive the desert, it was time to roll. Bolan got behind the wheel, following Azmeh's directions as they headed westward to Syria. Checkpoints at the border would have stopped them dead, but that was where the Jeep paid off, churning cross-country through the open desert toward the invisible line between countries.

3

Deir ez-Zor Governorate, Syria

Bolan hit the ground running, clutching his AKMS, using the Jeep's roiling dust cloud as cover. He tracked the charging truck by sound at first, then saw it looming through the gritty haze.

Never mind disabling the vehicle. The only way to stop or divert it, this close to impact, would be to nail the driver. Bolan stood his ground just long enough to aim a short burst at the dirt-streaked windshield, then he leaped and rolled aside before the hurtling juggernaut could crush him. He scrambled to his feet and fired another burst into the driver's door as it swept past him. The driver lurched and slumped, but Bolan couldn't tell how badly he was wounded, if at all.

Regardless, the truck was slowing down. Bolan dove back toward the Jeep, his only standing cover. Better for the Wrangler to absorb a few more rounds than for him to take a hit at such close range.

And guns were blazing now, no fewer than six or seven from the truck bed. To Bolan's left, Azmeh had joined the fight. As the dust began to settle, Bolan saw his adversaries jumping from the truck and scrambling for the cover of their own vehicle, firing wild bursts as they ran.

The truck was rolling on without them, slower by the moment. Finally, its motor hitched and stalled, most likely from a lack of gas while it was running in third gear. That meant no driver managing the clutch and stick shift. Bolan hoped he'd killed the stranger, but he wasn't taking it for granted.

He counted eight men on the ground, plus a shotgun rider in the cab. Make it ten if the driver was still fit for action.

When the truck died, it provided solid, stationary cover for his enemies. They couldn't rush him safely over the thirty yards of open ground between them, but they could snipe around the tailgate, across its hood, or wriggle underneath and try to sight him from a worm's-eye view.

The Jeep was taking hits now; time was on the opposition's side. Still, nothing had come close to nailing Bolan—yet.

If the enemy had a working radio, how long until reinforcements could arrive?

Azmeh was scuttling backward to the Jeep now, trading fire with hidden opponents. Their bullets kicked up spurts of dust and sand around his feet as he retreated. Bolan saw trouble coming, but he didn't want to call out and distract his comrade in the midst of battle.

Azmeh ran into the Wrangler's left-rear fender, grunting from the impact as he lost his balance and went down. The tumble saved him, as a well-aimed burst cut empty air where he'd been standing a second earlier. The bullets smacked into plastic fuel cans instead.

Bolan returned fire, pinning down the rifleman, while Azmeh rolled and crawled behind the Jeep. He wasn't safe, just covered for the moment.

Meanwhile, they were both pinned down.

"YOU MISSED HIM!" Sadek snarled, kicking one of Haaz Gemayel's legs where they protruded from beneath the truck. "What's wrong with you?"

Gemayel scooted backward, rising to his knees. He glared at Sadek, index finger on the trigger of his AK-47. "He fell down! That's not my fault, and I don't see you helping."

"I didn't have a clear shot," Sadek answered.

"Then get down here with the rest of us," Gemayel sneered before he ducked back under the truck.

That one was trouble, Sadek thought, a lazy bastard who defied authority when he believed he could get away with it. Why he had volunteered to fight in Syria remained a mystery.

Sadek had already lost one man. Sami Karam was dead or dying in the cab, struck by bullets through the windshield and another burst that had raked his door when Karam had failed to run his killer down. Sadek had bailed when the truck stalled, taking a moment to confirm that Karam wasn't moving before abandoning him.

At a time like this, if someone was not fit to fight, what good were they?

Sadek himself had yet to fire a shot since exiting the cab, but that was his prerogative as leader of the team.

He had been chosen to command and supervise, not do the dirty work himself. Of course, he'd killed before and would not hesitate to jump in if he had a clear shot at the enemy, but was it wise to risk a leader's life unnecessarily?

Sadek heard bullets strike the truck like hailstones, clanging into sheet metal. Someone cried out in pain under the chassis, a pair of legs thrashed briefly, then their owner started worming backward in fits and starts. Sadek was set to scold Bashar Alama when he emerged, face awash in blood, an ugly gash from a bullet graze above one eye.

"Youssef?" the wounded soldier asked. "Is that you? I can't see you."

Sadek fumbled for a handkerchief in his pocket, then pressed it into Alama's hand. "Wipe off your face," he said. "It's just a scratch. Each man must do his part."

"I will, but—"

"Be strong!" Sadek urged him, moving on before he had to answer any questions or fake a show of sympathy.

For his own sake, and for the estimation of his men, Sadek knew that he had to join the fight. But how? Rushing into the no-man's land between his truck and the old Jeep would be suicide, and he had never cherished dreams of martyrdom. For all he knew, one of his men might shoot him in the back before their common enemies could cut him down.

So, what else could he do?

He reached the front of the truck, where one of his young soldiers crouched and peered around the fender, straining for a glimpse of the enemy. Sadek tried to remember his name but drew a blank.

"What do you see?" he asked.

"Nothing," the young man replied. "They've gone to ground."

"We need to draw them out."

"Good luck with that," the soldier answered.

Sadek considered striking him for insolence, but then decided he had pushed his luck as far as it would go with these inexperienced, poorly trained guerrillas. Discipline was clearly fading in the ranks, the longer Syria's insurgency dragged on.

Sadek needed to make a grand, dramatic gesture to assert himself, to regain whatever measure of respect his men had felt for him before the shooting started and their nerve ran out. But what could he—

Of course!

There was an RPG-29 launcher lying behind his seat in the cab, with three rockets ready for loading. All he had to do was reach in, retrieve the ordnance while avoiding Karam's corpse, load the launcher, then take out his foes.

One step at a time, Sadek thought, as he returned to the door he had left hanging open. The Vampir and its ammo were in easy reach.

SABAH AZMEH SWITCHED out his empty AKMS magazine and snapped a full one in its place. His hip throbbed from his collision with the Jeep, a stupid, clumsy slip that made him feel like a fool even though it saved his life.

His jacket smelled strange, and he realized that gasoline had splashed on to his sleeve after he fell, one of their fuel cans punctured by the slugs that might have killed him otherwise. The stench stung Azmeh's nostrils and made his eyes water, but all that he could do was scoop up dirt in his free hand and rub it into his wet sleeve. He glanced at Cooper and found the tall American scowling at their predicament. Whatever he had planned, turning around to face the truck and stopping there, it was not working out. Unless he had hatched another scheme...

Cooper shifted, then walked over to the passenger door, keeping low. A burst of hostile fire drilled the Wrangler's bodywork, one slug caroming off the door near Cooper's head. He did not flinch as he leaned inside and rummaged through duffel bags. When he backed out, he was holding two grenades.

Each F1 "lemon," Azmeh knew, weighed a shade under one and a half pounds. A strong man could pitch one forty-five yards, remaining outside the grenade's estimated thirty-yard kill zone. But could Cooper drop one behind the stalled truck while under fire?

"How can I help you?" Azmeh asked, worried that Cooper might suggest he make the throw himself.

"Give me some cover," Cooper said. "I'll tell you when."

"Done."

Kneeling, one shoulder against the Jeep's sun-heated fender, Azmeh held his carbine ready, muzzle pointed at the pale blue sky, his finger on the trigger. Full automatic fire would empty his fresh magazine in four seconds flat, unless he controlled it. He'd go with short bursts to frighten his opponents and keep them from dropping Cooper in his tracks.

He waited, barely breathing, and had started feeling dizzy when the tall American said, "Now!"

BOLAN PULLED THE GRENADE'S pin and dropped the spoon as he began to move. He had about four seconds until detonation.

The opposition cut loose when he broke from cover, arm cocked for the pitch, an overhand fastball.

A bullet sliced at Bolan's sleeve, missing flesh and bone, as he dove back to cover in the Wrangler's shadow. There had been no time for him to follow the grenade in flight. He had to hope it did sufficient damage over there to let him make a second throw.

Bolan counted to three, then he heard the blast, followed by screams. No way for him to judge the damage without seeing it firsthand, but he knew pain when he heard it and the gargling sound of voices choked with blood.

How many dead or wounded out of the eight or ten they'd started with?

Still not enough.

Bolan switched the second F1 to his right hand and walked past Azmeh, staying low. "Good job on the first round. Time for number two."

His guide nodded. "I'm ready."

"On my 'go.'"

Another nod.

Bolan could tell fewer Kalashnikovs were on the job, but counting them by sound was hopeless. He would have a better feel for how many opponents he'd taken out when he stepped out into the open a second time.

He reached the Wrangler's rear end just as someone shot the spare tire into tatters on its tailgate mount. The Jeep already stank of leaking gasoline, its bodywork had turned into a sieve, and Bolan had his doubts about the old vehicle carrying them any farther on his desert mission. When the left-rear tire began to hiss, Bolan knew their ride was done.

It didn't matter, though. Survival was the first priority.

He glanced at Azmeh, rising from his crouch as he said, "Go!"

Azmeh was quicker this time, firing *through* the Wrangler—in one open window, out the other—at their adversaries. Bolan had the F1's pin free as he came around the tailgate, right arm drawing back—and saw one of the opposition sprinting out from cover, rushing toward him with the long tube of an RPG launcher across his shoulder.

"Watch it!" Bolan called to Azmeh, as he made his pitch and dove facedown into the dirt.

SADEK HAD STRUGGLED with the RPG-29 launcher, loading it from the rear with a TBG-29V thermobaric antipersonnel round as he sat on the hot, hard soil, praying that he got it right and was not about to kill himself, along with all the other men from his patrol.

Sadek was not a genius with technology, far from it. He could field strip, load and fire a fair variety of weapons, and he learned quickly when new ones fell into his hands. But he could not have said what *thermobaric* meant or how it worked, in scientific terms. He *had* seen its effects on vehicles and human flesh, a grisly sight replete with screams of agony from living targets as they fried and died. Sadek wished that upon his enemies today, after they had resisted and embarrassed him.

He would be satisfied, feel good about himself again,

when they had been reduced to blackened, shriveled husks upon the desert sand.

And he would be a hero then—if he could only find the will to rise and make his move.

That was the hard part, breaking cover under fire and facing down the enemy. Sadek was not a fan of open warfare, but he'd sworn an oath to Allah and his outcast people, which demanded sacrifice.

So be it.

Shouldering the RPG, he took a moment to adjust its $2.7\times1P38$ optical sight. There would be precious little time for aiming once Sadek had shown himself, but he would do his best and hope that it was good enough.

He had not told the others what he planned to do, preferring to surprise them after some had treated him with disrespect. Let those who questioned his authority be startled and amazed when he saved them. Anyone who challenged him from that point on would face Sadek's enduring wrath.

Or maybe they would laugh at him for failing, after he was dead. But then, it wouldn't matter.

Allah promised a reward for soldiers slain while serving Him. If these were to be Sadek's last moments, he would step willingly toward the open gates of Paradise.

Sadek lurched to his feet, struggling with the extra forty pounds balanced on one shoulder, then broke into a loping run. The moment he was visible, his enemies would do their best to kill him. Whether they succeeded was in Allah's hands. Sadek's job was to hold on long enough to aim and fire the thermobaric rocket, sending them to hell.

One of his soldiers shouted something after him, but

Sadek didn't catch it. Gaining speed, be broke around the front end of the truck and angled toward the bullet-riddled Jeep, in time to see one of his enemies coming out to meet him. The man was not firing at him, did not even have a gun in hand, but his right arm was cocked back...

Sadek understood too late. He knelt and tried to aim his RPG, just as an ovoid object dropped in front of him and wobbled forward, trailing wisps of smoke. A scream of rage had nearly reached his lips when the grenade exploded, switching off the lights in Sadek's world.

MACK BOLAN HIT the deck and rode out the explosion, heard the shrapnel buzzing overhead and off into the desert's dry infinity. When he opened his eyes, the runner with the RPG was gone—or, rather, most of him was gone. The F1 had exploded virtually in his lap, steel fragments ripping through his torso like a blender's blades and shredding him before he fell.

Dying, the guy had still managed to fire his launcher, but the rocket had been aimed skyward as shrapnel and the F1's shock wave had blown him backward. Whatever kind of round he'd loaded, it flew high and wide, arcing a quarter-mile into the clear blue, then descending several hundred yards behind the Jeep, where it erupted into oily flame on barren ground.

Bolan leaped to his feet and jerked his AKMS off its shoulder sling, charging the truck. His objective now was to catch the remainder of the team off balance as they ducked rounds from Azmeh's carbine and recovered from the explosion of his other frag grenade.

He charged around the truck's front end, firing before he had a clear target in sight. His enemies, some of them wounded, hadn't seen him coming, but they did their best—which wasn't good enough.

When all of the men were down and out, he called to Azmeh, then stood up and waved. The Arab came across to join him, cautiously eyeing the scattered dead, as if he thought they might be faking it.

When he was satisfied, Azmeh told Bolan, "They've destroyed the Jeep."

No big surprise there.

"Let's check out the truck," Bolan said.

He walked around and dragged the body out of the bloody driver's seat. He used the dead man's *keffiyeh* to mop up the blood, discarded it and slid behind the wheel.

It took a moment for the engine to turn over, but Bolan got it running on the second try. It sounded all right—no strange noises beneath the hood, no red lights on the dashboard. Bolan left it running as he climbed down from the cab and circled the truck with Azmeh, checking out the tires, peering underneath in search of leaks. The truck had taken hits, beginning with its windshield, and the right side was scarred with shiny shrapnel wounds, but nothing Bolan saw or heard gave any indication that the vehicle wouldn't go the distance.

"Better move our gear," he said, already heading toward the Jeep.

Bolan's mobile arsenal was still intact, tucked down against the rear floorboard. The transfer only took a moment, then he climbed back into the driver's seat, with Azmeh beside him.

He still didn't know exactly where they were going, other than the general direction, but they wouldn't have to walk.

At least, not yet.

4

Deir ez-Zor Governorate

Roger Segrest squinted at the blinding sun through his aviators, wishing he'd been smart enough to bring along a hat when he was packing for the trip to Syria. Of course, he'd planned on spending nearly all his time indoors, with air-conditioning, and hadn't given any thought at all to being shot out of the sky over a freaking desert in the middle of nowhere.

Next time, you'll know, he thought, and nearly laughed aloud. Just smiling hurt, with lips so dry and cracked. Another vital thing he'd forgotten: lip balm. And, of course, sunscreen.

The funny part was that there might not be a next time. He could die out here, from thirst, exposure, snakebite, take your pick. Rescuers, if they ever came, might find him mummified, a desiccated husk with insects living in his empty skull after they ate his shriveled brain. Maybe his friends at State would stick him in the Diplomacy Center Museum, assuming it ever got built. His wife could help them with the plaque.

Thinking of rescue troubled him and made him angry. They'd only been ninety minutes out of Baghdad when the plane went down, but here it was, day two, and still no help in sight. The worry came from knowing that all planes these days had emergency locator beacons on board, airliners usually packing more than one. The anger—most of it, at least—was currently directed at himself.

Segrest had been outfitted with a homing beacon of his own before he'd left DC. He'd put it in his suitcase, which had seemed like the best place for safekeeping until a rocket had ripped the guts out of their plane and left the baggage scattered God knew where.

Of course, the beacon hadn't been turned on. Why would it be?

"Stupid," Segrest muttered to himself.

"How's that, sir?" Walton asked him, standing at his elbow.

"Nothing, Dale. Forget it."

"Do you want some water?"

Did he ever! Segrest checked his wristwatch and shook his head. "Too early."

"I just thought—"

"No. Thank you."

After pulling the dead and wounded clear, doing what little could be done for the copilot, they had sorted through their supplies and rationed the bottled water found in the wreck. It just made sense, not knowing when they'd be picked up.

Or *if*, he added silently.

The pilot had been killed on impact; his sidekick

had a broken leg, an ugly compound fracture; and the flight attendant had gone flying when the rocket hit, slamming his skull against one of the overhead luggage containers. He'd drifted in and out of consciousness for a few hours, then he'd succumbed to his head injury.

And then, the goddamned storm had hit them out of nowhere. Tareq Eleyan had called it a haboob, and hearing that it was a fact of life in Syria had done nothing to lighten Segrest's mood while the dust and sand buried them, forcing them to dig out of the shattered plane a second time after they'd taken refuge there.

Segrest was worried about rescue, but that wasn't all. Someone had shot them down, either for sport or with intent. In either case, the shooter was still out there, likely to come looking for his prize and bringing friends along to pick over the wreckage. Segrest wished he knew who'd done it, what their motive was, and what he should expect when they showed up.

Not if, but when.

Trouble was coming. He could smell it on the breeze that kissed his blistered skin.

THE TRAITOR HAD a headache, a holdover from the crash that seemed beyond the reach of simple aspirin. He did not mind, particularly—life was mostly pain and disappointment, after all—but it annoyed him slightly, since he had been waiting for the rocket strike, strapped in when no one else had seat belts fastened, only to be struck a glancing blow from his own briefcase tumbling from the overhead compartment.

Irony. The spice of life.

He sat in the shade of the Let L 410's left wing, or what remained of it. At least three quarters of it had been sheared off on impact; it was still better than nothing, though the shade provided only minimal relief from the pervasive desert heat. But, then, what was discomfort when he'd been prepared to sacrifice his life?

There had been no schedule for the strike, no real way to prepare himself beyond keeping his seat belt fastened and pretending airplanes made him edgy.

Which, in this case, had been true.

He had been waiting for the blast, then plummeting to earth, uncertain whether he would die in the explosion or the crash. Imagining a midair detonation had been worse—well, *nearly* worse—than the reality when it occurred, but no one could suspect that he'd been waiting for it. His surprise had been absolutely genuine. His screams as they descended had been heartfelt.

But here he was, essentially unharmed besides the purpling bump on his forehead and the dull ache just behind his left eye socket. He was thirsty, like the rest of them, but that would pass when his comrades arrived and took the others into custody. He would be treated as a hero of the struggle then.

So, what was keeping them?

Another problem: since he didn't know exactly where the plane had been before the rocket strike, and he couldn't calculate how far they'd traveled afterward, he could not estimate the time required for his comrades to overtake them.

Truth be told, he wasn't even sure who would be coming for him; he had not been entrusted with that information, nor did he require it to complete his mission. After being shot out of the sky, his twofold task was simple.

First, deactivate the aircraft's homing beacons, following instructions he'd been given prior to takeoff. One had been eliminated by the rocket's blast; the other had been easy enough to disable in the chaos after touchdown.

Second—and only as a last resort—he was to kill his fellow passengers should the soldiers he expected fail to find the plane and round up the survivors. There was no precise deadline for that, but in his heart, the traitor reckoned he would know when it was time.

His tool, if it should come to that, would be a Liberator, the world's first fully 3D-printed gun, invented by Defense Distributed, a US firm whose blueprints were available online from various file-sharing websites. While the original gun was a single-shot model, the traitor carried a four-barrel pepperbox version in .380 ACP. Only the cartridges were metal, and their size made them easy to conceal inside common objects: an electric shaver and hair dryer, in his case.

He had eight rounds, total, but had already prioritized his targets, just in case he was disarmed before he could reload. If that happened, he would fight. Krav Maga was his specialty, and with any luck, he might be able to eliminate with his bare hands any enemy he failed to shoot.

Four rounds, five targets. He felt good about those odds.

"WE'VE LOST THEM, SIR," Aziz Zureiq declared.

"By design, Sergeant." Captain Nasser al-Kassar tried not to snap at his subordinate, but it was often difficult to curb his tongue. "A beacon would have brought Crusaders in to save them long before we reached the crash site."

"Yes, sir. But we don't know where the crash site is."

"We have their flight plan. That's enough for now."

Zureiq chose not to argue, thereby proving his intelligence. There was no reason for a lowly sergeant to share the captain's advance warning about the UN flight. Al-Kassar's superiors at Free Syrian Army headquarters had briefed him, told him that a mishap was expected, and assigned him to retrieve any survivors from the crash. They did not share their source of information or their motive for dispatching al-Kassar with thirty men to find the downed aircraft.

Why should they?

Granted, Captain al-Kassar had been confused by his assignment, more specifically the order to detain all those aboard the flight and treat them all as prisoners of war. One of the passengers, Muhammad Qabbani, was a well-known opposition spokesman and should logically have been regarded by the FSA as an ally. In fact, headquarters' gossip had it that the UN visitors were hoping to accelerate the removal of Syria's president. Why hold them captive, then, instead of speeding them along their way?

Captain al-Kassar knew it was not his place to ask such questions. And, in fact, he recognized his assignment to the mission as an honor, one that could result in his promotion if he pulled it off successfully, without embarrassing the FSA. Once he had climbed a little farther up the ladder, he'd be included in decision-making and could turn his mind to shaping policy.

Always assuming that the civil war continued.

Three years and counting, with no end in sight, and it occurred to him that certain leaders of the FSA might be reluctant for hostilities to cease. What would they do if the president was finally driven from his palace? Would they assume positions in whatever government displaced the current one, or would they just be cut adrift, no longer needed once the crisis was resolved? Would sane men act in concert to prolong the war, with all its suffering, simply to keep themselves employed?

The sergeant's voice cut through his gloomy thoughts. "Shall we move on, then, Captain?"

"Yes. Proceed, Sergeant."

Their little caravan—two Russian ZIL-131s, plus al-Kassar's staff car—was following the UN plane's projected flight path, hoping for some sign of it along the way. If they found nothing in the next twenty-four hours, he would have to speak with headquarters and ask for new instructions.

Which would look bad.

The captain said a silent prayer for help and trailed Sergeant Zureiq back to their vehicle.

Syrian Arab Army Headquarters, Damascus

COLONEL AREF JALLO snapped to attention, careful not to lock eyes with the man behind the broad, bare desk. "Reporting as instructed, General," he said.

Brigadier General Firas Mourad graced Jallo with a look of vague disdain and said, "At ease."

Jallo changed posture but did not relax. General officers unnerved him, and Mourad was known as one of the worst, capricious and vindictive, never one to overlook a slight—even imaginary ones—and quick to repay them tenfold.

"Your report, Colonel?" Mourad prodded.

Jallo swallowed a hard lump in his throat and said,

"Captain Fakhri reports no contact yet, sir. His unit is proceeding on the course provided, but—"

"But nothing," Mourad snapped, cutting him off. "They're looking for an aircraft large enough to carry nineteen people, downed in open desert, with the flight plan given to them in advance. It's white and bears the name of the United Nations. How hard can it be?"

"General, Captain Fakhri informs me that the area was swept by a haboob after the plane went down."

"Haboob," Mourad muttered. "A breeze."

"Sir, if you've never witnessed a storm like that."

"I come from Kobajjep," Mourad informed him. "Certainly, I've witnessed a haboob. Captain Fakhri has an assignment to complete. I am accepting no excuses if he fails. You made that clear?"

"Yes, sir!"

"And his response?"

"Of course, sir, he intends to carry out his mission as assigned. He observes, however—"

"More conditions, now?"

"Not a condition, General—an observation that when aircraft suffer damage during flight, they often deviate from their expected routes. Captain Fakhri has no way of knowing whether this plane remained on course, if it veered north or south—"

"I understand the concept, Colonel."

"Yes, sir. If I may say, in the absence of a homing beacon—"

"Stop explaining why the job cannot be done!" Mourad commanded. "You've been in the army long enough and risen high enough to understand procedures, have you not?"

"Yes, sir!"

"I issue orders. You transmit them. Captains and lieutenants carry out those orders. Understood?"

"Of course, sir." If Mourad believed he was superior to nature or the laws of physics, it was neither Jallo's place nor inclination to dispute him.

"You will contact Captain Fakhri and express dissatisfaction in the strongest terms. Remind him, if he has forgotten, that his rank is nothing carved in stone. Failure has consequences, and they're never pleasant."

"No, sir."

"It's a lesson I learned early. All subordinates should keep it foremost in their minds."

"Yes, sir."

"Dismissed!"

Jallo rose to attention once again, saluted, eyes fixed on the wall behind Mourad, a foot or so above his head. He pivoted and quick-marched to the door, drawing his next breath only when it closed behind him.

Jallo knew the basics of the mission that was giving Mourad fits and threatening a young captain's career. A UN plane had been shot down, and Captain Fakhri had been sent to find its passengers, collect them and await further instructions. Jallo was not sure what that meant, but he did not altogether like the sound of it.

His homeland was in chaos, seething from within, harangued from every side by other, larger nations who believed they had the right to mold domestic policy. Jallo was no great fan of the president, but he had sworn an oath to serve his country. He was not a mutineer, would not forsake the service that had been his home since he enlisted at eighteen. Whatever history decided was the better course for Syria, Jallo had orders to transmit and to obey.

Deir ez-Zor Governorate

"YES, SIR. I UNDERSTAND completely," Captain Bassam Fakhri said. He gripped the sat phone tightly, to prevent it from slipping out of his sweaty palm.

"And no excuses," Colonel Jallo cautioned.

"No, sir. Only positive results."

"We all hope so."

"Colonel, shall I continue to report if…there is nothing to report?"

"By all means, Captain. But to me directly, no one else."

"Yes, sir."

The line went dead, and Fakhri set the phone aside.

"They're hounding you," Sergeant Ilyas Malki said.

"Naturally. We've fallen behind schedule, disappointing some important people."

"On a simple rescue mission," Malki said. "What does headquarters care about the UN, anyway? They smother us with sanctions for attempting to defend ourselves, then call us criminals if we avoid their illegal blockades. To hell with them!"

The sergeant never failed to speak out in support of the president. Fakhri agreed with him in principle, had followed certain orders in the past that made him cringe a bit inside, and knew which side his bread was buttered on. Defeat meant death or exile for staff officers connected to what foreign journalists habitually called "atrocities." War, by its very definition, was atrocious, and the critics of his homeland did not seem to understand who'd started this one, which unwelcome outsiders had kept it going on for years.

"Let's just do the job and be done with it," he advised the sergeant.

"All I mean to say is—"

"Yes, I heard you. Have the men fall in. We're leaving now."

"Yes, sir."

Fakhri would keep on searching, hoping to detect a signal from the downed aircraft. Without it, he supposed the hunt might carry on for days, each fresh report with no results another nail in the casket of his career. Colonel Jallo seemed like a reasonable officer, but there were others high above him who would not forget a failure or forgive the man they deemed responsible.

Eventually, Fakhri knew, he would locate the UN plane. If it had, in fact, fallen from the sky within the area assigned to him, discovery must be inevitable. He might spend the next five years searching for its remains, but somehow, someday...

No. His impatient superiors demanded *swift* results, and failure to provide them would mean transfer to an active battle area, perhaps demotion to a lower rank. It was unlikely he would face a court-martial, but given the current atmosphere at headquarters...

"Captain!" The shout came from a corporal, hunched in the open doorway of a BTR-152 armored personnel carrier. "Captain Fakhri!"

"What is it?"

"The beacon, sir. I've found it!"

"What?"

It seemed irrational, impossible. They had been scanning for the signal since they'd left the city, without result. Why should they suddenly detect it now?

"Explain," Fakhri commanded.

"I cannot, sir," said the corporal, sheepishly. "One moment I was scanning and had nothing. Then…see for yourself."

Fakhri took the scanner, glaring at it. The soldier was correct. They had a signal on the proper frequency, beckoning more or less in the correct direction, north-northeast.

"How far away is that?" he asked the corporal.

"Approximately thirty miles, sir."

"Very good." He turned and shouted to the other men, "Hurry! We're wasting time!"

Fakhri supposed that he should phone Colonel Jallo and update his report, but what if this turned out to be a false alarm? A flashing light and pinging noise were nothing, in the scheme of things. No, he would wait until he had the aircraft's passengers in hand, then log his next report.

Whatever happened after that, he was a soldier pledged to follow orders.

Let the hunt resume.

SANI BANKOLE WORE a blue baseball cap with the United Nations emblem embroidered in white on its crown. Pulled low, the bill shaded his face, but the sun beat down on the rest of him, causing him to sweat through his white dress shirt.

He could survive the heat, of course. It wasn't sun that worried him.

Bankole saw Roger Segrest standing with his aide and went to join them, making sure they witnessed his approach and would not think he planned on eavesdropping. Experience had taught him that suspicion was a fact of life with diplomats; they were always alert to subterfuge and double-dealing, whether they were trying to negotiate a cease-fire between mortal enemies or simply passing idle time with friends.

The news he carried now was bound to put Segrest's suspicion into overdrive.

Bankole waited for the two Americans to notice him and break off their discussion. When he had the State Department undersecretary's full attention, he asked, "May we speak together privately?"

Segrest frowned, his eyes invisible behind his sunglasses. "Of course," he said, after a moment's hesitation. "Dale, excuse us, will you?"

The aide smiled and complied.

When there was no one else to hear, Bankole got directly to the point. "I've had a conversation with the copilot," he said. "About our homing beacons."

"And?"

"He gave me their location. One, it seems, was either lost or obliterated when the rocket struck. The other is inside the cockpit, attached to the flight recorder."

"Okay..."

"The cockpit beacon has an on-off switch," Bankole said. "It's deactivated on arrival at the aircraft's destination, then turned on before the next departure."

Segrest nodded. "And your point is?"

"I found ours turned off."

Tight-lipped, Segrest replied, "One of the pilots?"

"No. As you know, one died on impact and the other was disabled. He denies deactivating it, in any case. I cannot fathom any motive he might have to leave us stranded here, particularly since his life may hinge on rescue."

"Who is he? Where's he from?"

"A commercial pilot from New York. His firm is one of many on retainer to the UN. It is most unlikely that he could have known our mission, much less placed himself in a position to become involved."

Segrest blew out a breath and turned to glower at the other members of their party, who were huddled more or less together in the meager shadow of their wrecked, half-buried plane. "You're saying that we've got a mole."

"A traitor in our midst," Bankole said. "It would appear so, yes."

"About the beacon…"

"I turned it back on. It's functioning."

"Okay, so help is coming."

"Theoretically," Bankole said. "In time."

"And while we're waiting, all we have to do is find the traitor," Segrest said. "At least we've got it narrowed down to three."

"You would include my aide?" Bankole asked.

"He's Arab," Segrest said.

"Jordanian. And is your aide excluded from the suspect list?"

"Dale? Hey—"

"And then, what of ourselves?" Bankole asked.

"You're serious?"

"Why not?"

"I know *I* didn't do it," Segrest answered. "And you just told me about the beacon."

"Perhaps I was afraid it would be found out, otherwise."

"And now you've called for help?"

"Unless I've lied about that, too."

"I guess I'd better see that beacon for myself," Segrest replied. "You lead the way."

5

The truck died moments after Bolan locked on to the downed plane's homing beacon on his GPS reader. They were rolling over flat ground one minute, the next, stopped dead without a warning. Bolan scanned the dashboard for red light, pumped the clutch, and tried again.

Nothing.

He climbed down from the cab and walked around to pop the hood. He was a passable mechanic, good enough to keep most auto engines running if he had the parts and tools, but what he saw beneath the truck's hood was beyond his skill set. In their firefight with the truck's first owners, a round had bored through the fender and clipped a cable linking the battery to the truck's alternator. All the time they'd been driving, they had been running down the battery without recharging it.

"I can't fix this," he told Azmeh, who'd joined him to investigate. "I'd need another cable and a jump start. We're not going anywhere in this."

He dropped the hood with a resounding, final clang.

"So, what now?" Azmeh inquired.

"We've found the beacon signal," Bolan said. "We can't stop now. Looks like we walk."

"How far?"

"About a hundred sixty miles."

"So, about fifty hours, if we keep up our pace and don't take breaks," Azmeh observed.

Two days, at best, but likely more, since the heat would slow them down. No good. A thousand things could happen to the stranded diplomats in that time.

"We need another ride," Bolan said.

"Yes," Azmeh concurred. "We need another ride. Where might we obtain one?"

Bolan stared far into the distance, focusing on the general direction of the homer that had been reactivated moments earlier. "Job one," he said, "we stay the course. No deviations from the signal unless we spot something, someplace, where we're likely to pick up another vehicle."

"Agreed," Azmeh replied, without a trace of hesitation. "But if there is no vehicle to be found?"

Bolan appreciated Azmeh's calm and the fact that he did not suggest calling for help. The truck contained no radio, and Bolan's only sat-phone link was to an office halfway round the world, in Washington, DC. Any assistance Brognola could provide would take hours, at least, and they'd lose more time waiting for a replacement vehicle than they would in walking toward the beacon's flashing light.

Another problem: there was no one in the country they could trust. If they *did* find someone who had a working car, they'd likely have to steal it. That would raise the possibility, however slim, of a police pursuit.

Bolan did not dwell on the setbacks. From the truck, he fetched the Dragunov, one of their ammo bags and the RPG-7, wrestling them all on to slings. Azmeh took the RPK, a second ammo bag and the launchers' rockets. Heavy laden, both men turned their faces north and started walking at a steady, numbing, ground-eating pace.

One hundred and sixty miles? It might as well have been a thousand, but the Executioner had no choice. Quitting wasn't in him. He would press on till he dropped, and then, if he was still alive, he'd start to crawl.

ROGER SEGREST CLEARED his throat and used a handkerchief to blot some of the perspiration from his forehead, then returned it to his pocket.

"If I could please have everyone's attention for a moment," he called out, waiting while the other crash survivors wrapped up their conversations and turned toward him.

"Thank you," he pressed on, once everyone was quiet. "I just have a quick announcement, which I hope you'll think is good news."

Here and there, an eyebrow rose. "It turns out," he said, "that when we crashed, our emergency locator beacon got turned off somehow. Maybe the impact of our landing did it. That's why nobody's come looking for us yet. Between the beacon cutting out and damage to the radio, we're off the grid."

He let that sink in, scanning the five faces, waiting for the mole to give himself away by any small gesture or sudden change in expression. Segrest had conceived the plot with Bankole, aware of the risk. It seemed like the only way they could possibly unmask the traitor. As to what action he might take from that point onward, he had no plan.

"So, that's the bad news," Segrest told them. "And the *good* news is, I've turned the locator back on again. They'll pick us up in Baghdad now, and probably in Deir ez-Zor. One way or another, someone should be coming for us fairly soon."

The questions started then. Dale Walton raised his hand, just like a kid in school, but started talking at the same time. "I thought those black box things were supposed to be unbreakable. How could it just switch off?"

"Beats me," Segrest replied. "It's possible one of the crew forgot to turn it on at takeoff, but we can't exactly ask them now."

As Segrest spoke, he nodded toward the copilot, stretched out against the airplane's fuselage. The poor guy was out of it, delirious with pain and what Segrest supposed must be the onset of an infection that would kill him if they didn't get help soon.

Walton wasn't satisfied, but he took Segrest's answer as the best he was going to get. Muhammad Qabbani spoke up next. "I wonder who else might respond now, to the beacon?" he inquired.

Segrest was ready with an answer, sketched out in advance to light a fire under the mole. "It's doubtful any of the opposition forces have equipment to pick up the homing beacon," he replied. "I could be wrong, of course. The military likely has something, for tracking down their own planes if they crash. The good news is, they're not supposed to know we're coming."

Not supposed to, but almost certainly did.

"Are we safe here?" Qabbani asked him.

"I won't lie to you," Segrest replied. "I'm hoping that relief comes in from Baghdad. They can get us out, and we can try rescheduling the meeting. If the army shows up first, well, we could have a problem."

That was Bankole's cue. "There is no need for fear. I feel certain they will respect diplomatic immunity."

"That's no help to me or Rafic," Qabbani answered back. "To them we're all just rebels. Outlaws."

"We'll just have to keep our fingers crossed," said Segrest, wondering what must be going on inside the traitor's mind.

NASSER AL-KASSAR FELT optimistic for the first time since he had been assigned to lead the search for Muhammad Qabbani and the others. He had worried, from the outset, that they all might have been killed when they were shot out of the sky. That would have foiled the plan devised by his superiors—as would failure to find the downed aircraft at all.

Now, by some miracle, the plane's locator beacon had begun to function, nearly two full days after the crash. Al-Kassar did not know why it had been silent all that time, or why it had begun to work just now— perhaps Allah had intervened somehow—but he was grateful for the break and meant to take advantage of it to the fullest.

Sergeant Zureiq's voice cut into his thoughts. "If I may ask you, Captain, what are we supposed to do with all those people?"

"That has yet to be decided," said al-Kassar. He was a bit surprised how easily the lie came to his lips.

"I only wondered if this was supposed to be a rescue mission, or…"

Zureiq did not finish the sentence but left it hanging as if he expected al-Kassar to complete if for him. Deftly sidestepping the trap, al-Kassar replied, "My orders are to find them and secure them. From that point, Idlib will decide."

The FSA's commanders had been headquartered in the capital of Idlib Governorate for several years. In fact, the decision had already been made, but it was not something al-Kassar planned to share, at this point, with a lowly sergeant. When the time came, he would issue orders, not debate the matter with his men.

"The brigadiers are wise, of course," Zureiq allowed. Two generals shared command of the FSA with a colonel, rotating service as commander in chief. "They understand that we have friends aboard the plane, I'm sure."

"No doubt," al-Kassar agreed. The conversation was beginning to annoy him.

"Do we have a plan, Captain, in case we reach the site too late?"

"Too late for what?" Al-Kassar pictured the passengers stretched out beside their aircraft, corpses baking in the desert sun.

"Well, others may be seeking them as we are, eh? The army, Hezbollah, who knows? What happens then?"

"We shield them from all harm, at any cost," al-Kassar replied. "Those are my orders. In the meantime, pray that we are first to find them, all alive and well."

"I will, Captain. May Allah hear and heed our prayers."

Al-Kassar turned from the sergeant, peering through

the open window of his staff car at the endless desert. Soldiers would be eating dust behind him, in the BTR-50 armored personnel carrier and in the Ural 375D trucks. All three of the vehicles had been captured from regular army outposts—liberated, as it were—and they would serve well in the final execution of his secret order.

Execution. Yes, that was the word.

The video performance that he had in mind would be sensational—and it would cost the animal at the head of the regime whatever marginal support he still enjoyed outside of Syria. Americans were fond of saying all was fair in love and war.

Captain Nasser al-Kassar would soon be testing that hypothesis.

THIS WILL BE the death of me, Sabah Azmeh decided. Someday in the distant future, some nomad will find my bones, perhaps my weapons also, and he'll wish he knew what madness had brought me here.

Or maybe, he'd just steal the guns.

Azmeh had no idea how far they had walked since the Russian truck died. The hard-baked soil beneath his feet burned like a bed of coals, searing him through the thick soles of his boots. His legs felt wooden, almost numb. His camouflage fatigues were soaked with sweat. The straps that crisscrossed Azmeh's torso chafed his shoulders raw, striking new sparks of pain each time they shifted by a fraction of an inch. His throat was parched, and breathing was an exercise in agony.

A few yards ahead of him, Matt Cooper seemed to bear the torture well enough. His own fatigues were dark with sweat, but otherwise, he might have just begun a stroll across some sylvan glen, with fragrant blooms and burbling brooks on either side. Azmeh began to wonder if the man was human, or a cyborg warrior sent from some top-secret lab to test its capabilities in battle.

Insane, he thought. The sun has baked my brain. I've lost my mind.

But he was still upright, still plodding forward through the heat haze. What alternative was there? He could walk on, or lie down where he was and die.

The homing beacon ruled them. Cooper had his GPS device locked on it, and he obviously had no plans to waver from the shortest, most direct course they could manage. So far, that forced march had not brought them to shade or water. As for how much longer he could follow Cooper without dropping in his tracks, Azmeh had no idea.

Suddenly, as if responding to that thought, Cooper stopped dead. He pointed forward, slightly to his left. "A house." It reassured Azmeh, somehow, to hear the tall American's voice croak.

Azmeh looked for the house, missed it at first, then thought it might be nothing but a mirage. At last, he realized it was real. A house in the middle of nowhere. And more importantly, he caught a gleam of sun on metal near the structure.

A water tank? A vehicle? Azmeh would welcome either one, and if it proved to be some useless object, he would settle for the shade a building offered. If they were forced to claim that shade by force, Azmeh supposed it would not weigh too heavily upon his conscience.

"How far is it, do you think?" he rasped, his throat like sandpaper.

"Maybe a quarter mile," Cooper replied. "No more than half."

Six hundred steps, at least, the way his feet were dragging now, perhaps eleven hundred. It was daunting, might have made him weep if he had any moisture left to spare, but it was *something*, an objective, possibly a ray of hope.

"It's probably abandoned," he told Cooper.

"Only one way to find out."

Azmeh nodded, causing pain to flare up from his aching neck and into his temples. Cooper led the way, and Azmeh followed, wondering if this was but a detour en route to hell.

CAPTAIN FAKHRI CONSULTED his GPS once again, mouthing a silent curse as his staff car jolted over rugged ground. "Be careful, Sergeant!" he commanded. "We don't need a broken axle here."

"No, sir," Malki replied, his voice bland. "Shall I slow down, sir?"

"No!" Fakhri retorted, even as he recognized the contradiction. "Simply be more careful."

"Yes, sir."

Fakhri hated it when Malki humored him. It made him want to slap the crusty little noncom, which would be a major breach of military etiquette. Instead, he sat and fumed, wondering why his GPS did not reveal his little convoy making better progress toward their target.

Of course, there were no highways in this portion of the eastern desert, only camel tracks and unpaved roads that blew away each time a sandstorm passed.

His party was trailblazing, traveling by what appeared to be the shortest route available, but still too far away to suit him.

What if someone else was following the aircraft's homing beacon? Fakhri would never hear the end of it if a United Nations rescue party crossed the border from Iraq and snatched the interlopers before he could take them into custody. There must be rebel forces in the area as well, though he had no idea if any of them knew about the so-called diplomats' trip. Outsiders always claimed to know how other nations should conduct political affairs and treat their dissidents. They remained safe at home in distant lands while they gave orders, strangling Syria with economic sanctions.

Captain Fakhri, as a respected military officer, would have no part of such subversive schemes. He had sworn an oath to uphold the Syrian state and its new constitution, established in 2012, which any fool could recognize as the most liberal document in his homeland's history. Where else did common Arabs have so many civil liberties?

The next time Fakhri checked his GPS, he saw that they *were* gaining on their stationary target, after all. The distance left to travel still disturbed him, but he guessed that they could reach the crash site in ninety minutes, maybe even an hour, if they held their present speed and met no opposition or obstructions on the way.

Fakhri was looking for the aircraft's passengers, not simply the plane itself. He hoped to find at least a few of them alive, but corpses could be useful in their own way, offered up as evidence of territorial incursion by the US and United Nations. The president could place the dead on trial via the internet; he could protest to UN headquarters, for all the good that it would do, and Russia might take up the case if all else failed.

The main thing was to find the infiltrators, make sure none had slipped away and take them into custody if they were still alive. That done, he would await instruction from headquarters in Damascus, and obey whatever orders he received.

Would it be life or death for the invaders?

Captain Fakhri thought about it and decided that it made no difference to him.

THE OLD, RAMSHACKLE house was not abandoned. Rather, Bolan saw as they approached, it was the centerpiece of a small and struggling farm. Sugar beets seemed to be the main crop, with some olive trees clinging tenaciously to life. The farmer saw them coming, well out from the house, and met them on his front porch with an old Lee-Enfield rifle.

The last thing Bolan needed was a shoot-out with some complete stranger who might have a family waiting inside the old house.

The farmer called them to a halt at fifty yards. Azmeh translated the exchange while Bolan scanned the property. The gleam of metal they'd observed from far off was, in fact, a vehicle—a purple, late-fifties era Cadillac Sixty Special, complete with phony air scoops. It was polished to perfection, shaded by a leaning carport, but it wouldn't hold the small crowd Bolan was hoping to retrieve.

"He asks if we are soldiers, and for which side," Azmeh said.

"Tell him the truth. We're on a rescue mission."

Azmeh passed it on and translated the farmer's quick reply. "Who needs rescuing?"

"Wayward travelers," said Bolan.

And the farmer answered, through Azmeh, "Why so many weapons, then?"

"Syria's dangerous these days," Bolan replied. "As you know very well."

The farmer almost cracked a smile at that but caught it in the nick of time. "What do you want from me?" he asked in Arabic.

"We need a vehicle. Though not this precious Cadillac."

The farmer mulled it over, then called out a name. A boy of about twelve or thirteen emerged, holding a double-barreled shotgun from another century. The old man issued rapid-fire orders, then stepped down off the porch and started toward the west side of the house, leaving the boy to follow up and cover them.

Around in back, there sat a Ford Ranchero pickup of the same vintage as the Caddy, rusted out in spots, with a long diagonal crack across its windshield. One headlight was missing from its socket, but the tires seemed to be holding air.

"Does it run?" Bolan asked.

The farmer answered Azmeh's translated question by producing a single key and tossing it to Bolan. Bolan caught it, eased into the driver's seat, and pumped the pedal twice before he turned the key. Beneath the truck's speckled hood, a Ford straight-six engine growled to life, belching through a hole in the Ranchero's muffler. The cab would only seat two people, but the pickup's open bed could take a full load, if and when they found the stranded diplomats.

"How much?" asked Bolan. Azmeh came back with a well-inflated asking price.

The pickup's fuel gauge needle stood at full, but how long would that last? "Tell him I'll double that," Bolan said, "if he throws in extra gas and then forgets he ever saw us."

That produced a gap-toothed smile. The farmer nodded, barking orders to his young backup, while Bolan climbed out of the Ford and started counting bills into the old man's calloused hand.

6

The traitor focused on remaining calm, avoiding any careless word or nervous tic that might betray him. He had half expected pointing fingers when the sunburned Crusader announced he'd reactivated the aircraft's homing beacon. He had calculated the distance from the spot where he was sitting to the bag that held his pistol, but no one called him out or even looked askance at him.

That bought some time, but not too much. There was no deadline for arrival of the FSA squad he expected to collect the infiltrators, but resumption of the beacon's broadcast meant he had to be alert, watching for anyone who might approach the plane, ready to strike if they were regulars, nomadic traders, bandits—anyone at all, besides his comrades.

After the American's announcement, he'd engaged in small talk with the others, voicing gratitude that they might soon be saved. Once he had made the rounds, he drifted back inside the aircraft's cabin, braving the kiln-like heat, to retrieve his bag. It was a moment's work to open it, extract the 3D-printed pistol, and conceal it underneath the loose tail of his shirt. Another moment, and he had the shaver open, spilling extra rounds into his palm and slipping them into his pocket.

Ready.

Emerging from the plane, he glanced about to see if anyone was watching him and found them all distracted by the news they'd just received. Sani Bankole and the top American, Segrest, were huddled near the LET's crumpled nose, heads close together as they spoke in whispers.

Clearly, they knew someone had shut the beacon off; or did they truly think it might have been forgotten during takeoff from Baghdad? The traitor could not trust that. For his own sake, he must treat his enemies as if they all suspected him and were preparing even now to move against him.

When that move came, from a single foe or all of them at once, he would not hesitate.

The Liberator pepperbox was simple to operate, but it had no sights, so shots would only be effective at close range. Point-blank was best, if he could manage it. His pistol rounds were subsonic hollow points in .380 caliber. On impact with flesh, the bullets flared to create a sharp petal shape that inflicted maximum damage.

Head shots were guaranteed fatalities.

The traitor was considering how long to wait, where he should be positioned for his first shot, when the second-string American cried out, "Look! The dust! Somebody's coming!"

The traitor turned with all the rest, followed the young man's pointing finger toward a dust cloud on the southwestern horizon. Judging distances was dif-

ficult out here. A nomad likely could have estimated it
to the meter, but the traitor was a city boy at heart. To
him, the rising dust plume might have been five miles
away, or twenty.

It was visible and drawing closer. That was all that
mattered.

Friends or foes?

Reaching around to touch the concealed pistol, he
resolved to wait and see.

BASSAM FAKHRI WOULD not have seen the aircraft—or
what was left of it—without the beacon guiding him
to its location. Even within a hundred yards of where it
lay, the outline of its fuselage was still obscured by sand
from the recent storm, its open doors mere shadows on
the landscape, easily mistaken for the mouths of caves.

Fakhri saw six men standing more or less in line
along the left side of the plane, watching his small convoy approach. One more lay off to the side, beneath a
blanket that had been erected as a makeshift tent, to
give him shade. The prostrate man had obviously worn
a uniform before the crash: he still had on the white
shirt, with epaulets. His black trousers had been slit to
bare a badly broken leg that someone had tried to splint.

A crewman, then—no one who concerned Captain
Fakhri.

He did not recognize the others as his staff car
stopped in front of them. Fakhri had been informed of
their intentions, and he'd been given the orders to capture them, alive if possible. What happened to them
after that depended on the instructions he received once
they were in his custody.

Stepping from his vehicle with one hand on his holstered Makarov, Fakhri waited for Sergeant Malki to join him, hearing his soldiers unload from their truck and the BTR-152. Atop the armored personnel carrier, one private kept the NSV heavy machine gun trained on the raggedy survivors of the plane crash.

Two of them stepped forward now. One of them spoke, his accent suggesting a West African background. "Good afternoon, and welcome," he began, smiling. "We have been hoping someone would arrive to help us."

"Help you?" Captain Fakhri answered, with a musing tone. "We have been ordered to arrest you for invading the Syrian Arab Republic. You will come with us to answer charges before the State Security Court."

"Invading?" Now it was the other man's turn to speak. He was obviously an American, accustomed to respect no matter how he trampled on the laws of other nations. "You're making a serious—"

The other man turned to him and muttered something, cutting off the rude tirade. When he turned back to Fakhri, he was all smiles once again. "I am afraid there has been a misunderstanding. We are delegates from the United Nations and the United States, attempting to resolve—"

"You are trespassers," Fakhri interrupted him. "Meddlers and enemies of our leader. It does not matter who you represent, since you have entered Syria without permission or approval from our government."

The African was fighting to retain his smile. "But we—"

"And *this* one," Fakhri cut him off again, pointing to one man halfway down the line, "is *not* from the United Nations or United States. He is Muhammad Qabbani.

I recognize him from the posters charging him with treason, terrorism and subversion."

"We have diplomatic immunity," the African answered, his expression now somber. "Please examine our credentials."

"Forgeries, no doubt. And none of that applies to enemies found sneaking over borders. You will come with us. A judge will study your so-called credentials at his leisure."

The American could hold his tongue no longer. "I'm an officer of the US State Department," he declared. "I demand a phone line to contact my embassy."

Fakhri stepped closer to the man, his right hand still resting on the Makarov. "If you are wise," he said, "you will remember that you are in no position to make demands. Now, all of you! Into the truck!"

The African glanced toward the man lying beneath the makeshift tent. "Our pilot has been badly injured. He needs medical assistance."

"Say goodbye to him," Fakhri advised. "You have no need for pilots now."

BOLAN'S GPS TOLD HIM they had eighty-seven miles to go before they reached whatever still remained of the United Nations plane. He still had no idea why there had been no beacon in the first phase of his search or why its function had resumed. Both circumstances fueled suspicion, but his top priority was getting to the crash site and finding out if anyone was still alive.

"Will they all fit in the back?" Azmeh asked when they'd put the lonely farm behind them.

"I suppose they'll have to," Bolan answered. "For a few miles, anyway."

The last part of his plan was simple enough in concept: collect the crash survivors, drive them east toward the border, far enough to make them safe from any incoming patrols, then call for air support. Although the US military had officially withdrawn from Iraq, America still had personnel in the country who would send choppers to lift the diplomats, Bolan and Sabah Azmeh out of Syria.

But he'd be surprised if it went that smoothly.

The farm was thirty miles behind them, or a little more, when Bolan saw the vehicles ahead, sitting beside the whisper of a camel track that they were following northeastward. Azmeh saw them as well, murmured a curse, then said, "A checkpoint."

"When's the last time that you saw a checkpoint in the middle of the desert, with no road or border anywhere close by?" Bolan inquired.

"You're right. Bandits, then."

Or stragglers, Bolan thought, maybe deserters from one of the various guerrilla outfits operating inside Syria. Smart money said the people waiting up ahead would all be armed, less interested in his nationality or travel papers than in grabbing anything of value they could steal, before they executed him and Azmeh on the spot.

"You going to drive around them?" Azmeh asked, not sounding hopeful.

"Wouldn't work," said Bolan. They'd already been in one wild chase across the desert, lost their Wrangler in the process, and he knew the old Ranchero wouldn't survive a similar experience. "Be ready when I make my move."

"I will," said Azmeh, clearly not encouraged by the prospect.

NASSER AL-KASSAR PEERED into the aircraft's interior, hot light streaming in through both open doors. The only person still inside the plane was clearly dead, up in the cockpit. Outside, only one remained, and he was incoherent, raving through the fever that consumed him.

"We've missed them, Captain," Zureiq said, not helpful in the least.

"I see that, Sergeant. Thank you."

Stepping back into full sunlight, still cooler than the cabin with its stagnant air of death, al-Kassar surveyed the site. Where had his targets gone? He saw the marks of big tires, where at least two vehicles had turned before proceeding northward.

Army? Someone else?

He approached the dying man and knelt beside him, ducking underneath his blanket tent, peering into his fevered eyes. Whatever blight was raging through his system, it was not contagious. The infection in his shattered leg had swollen it enough to strain the strips of blanket used to bind his splint. A surgeon might have saved his life by amputation, but al-Kassar's team had no doctor, and he did not have the time to spare.

He slapped the crewman's dripping face, lightly at first, then using greater force to make his eyes focus. "Need…help," the man said.

"I see that," al-Kassar answered, using rusty English. "I can help you, but I need an answer first."

"Answer?"

"Where have the others gone?"

"Others?"

"From the plane. Who took them?"

"Soldiers."

"Regulars?"

"Need…help," the crewman said again.

Al-Kassar gave up. In his demented state, the man would not know one group of armed men in fatigues from any other.

"Help you shall have," al-Kassar said, as he rose and backed away. "Sergeant, help him."

Zureiq blinked at him, then replied, "Yes, sir" and drew his pistol. He leaned in, aimed and fired once into the crewman's skull, ending his earthly misery. The dead man shivered, his good leg kicking, while the other merely wobbled in its clumsy splint.

"We have a trail to follow," said al-Kassar, "before the desert blows it all away."

And how long would that be? He was so close to victory, and now it might be snatched away from him. Bitterness made al-Kassar spit into the sand beneath his boots.

He had nearly reached his staff car, was about to mute the nagging GPS device clipped to his belt, when it picked up a second pinging sound. Snatching the reader, al-Kassar saw a second dot moving north from the stationary beacon of the plane. He tried to judge the distance on the small screen, guessing that the second beacon—and whoever carried it—had traveled ten to fifteen miles from the crash site.

They were within his reach if al-Kassar moved quickly enough.

"Back to the vehicles!" he shouted at his men. "Hurry!"

Eight men were waiting at the "checkpoint," four for each of the two clapped-out European SUVs they had arrived in. Bolan recognized a Russian Niva and a Ro-

manian Dacia Duster, both of them sandblasted, show-
ing their age with rust spots, dents and dings, cracked
windshields, balding tires.

The men weren't much to look at, either. Two were
fairly stout, the rest slender, their varied heights a dis-
cordant musical scale. They were dirty and unkempt,
but their weapons, on the other hand, were polished
and clean. They held various models of Kalashnikovs,
loaded with curved banana clips, ready to rock and roll.

Bolan slowed on the approach and let the gunmen
see him looking at them through the Ford Ranchero's
windshield. Casually, carefully, he raised the AKMS
to his lap, keeping it down below the dashboard and
the steering wheel, while Azmeh did likewise. Their
windows were already down, and both auto rifles were
ready with fresh magazines. Once Bolan checked his
safety, he was good to go.

"We don't have time to bargain with them," he told
Azmeh. "The second their weapons come up, take them
down as quickly as you can."

"Will they not have us in a cross fire?" Azmeh asked.

"That's their first mistake," Bolan replied, and smiled.

At thirty yards, the gunmen started fanning out a
bit, but not enough to matter. They were trying to in-
timidate Bolan and Azmeh, cow them from the start
to make things easy on themselves. Fear gave them an
advantage.

They were in for a surprise.

At fifteen yards, still smiling, Bolan asked the shooters on his side of the Ranchero, "What's up, guys?"

One of the paunchy ones replied in Arabic, and Bolan
nodded in phony understanding. He heard the click of a

safety as Azmeh said something to the men on his side of the car. Go time.

Bolan hit the one who'd spoken to him with a three-round burst, center mass, and blew him back into the sand.

And then, all hell broke loose.

Azmeh was firing from his window, short bursts, while his targets tried to scramble. Bolan focused on his own remaining adversaries, who were ducking, dodging, not as ready for resistance as they'd thought they were.

He caught the second shooter raising his Kalashnikov and stitched him with a burst around belt level, gutting him. The scrawny guy collapsed but still managed to fire a few rounds skyward as he died.

Two left, and they were both diving for cover, counting on their SUV to shield them from incoming fire while they regrouped. It might have worked, if Bolan was intent on blowing past their roadblock in a cloud of dust, but he'd already shifted the Ranchero into park and had his door open, pursuing them.

When one of them peeked up to find out what was happening, Bolan obliged him with a round between the shiny lenses of his shades. The fourth man saw his partner die and must have gotten some on him in the process. When he lunged forward, roaring, firing aimlessly, his face was smeared with blood along one side, making him look as if he'd already been shot. Reality caught up with first impressions a half second later, as a double-tap smashed through his snarling face and finished him.

Bolan reversed direction, just in time to see Azmeh's last adversary fall, clutching his throat with bloody hands. Bolan checked the SUVs, deciding that the Niva was their best bet for continuing their journey over rugged ground. The bonus was a stash of loaded AK magazines, same caliber as their weapons, and six spare cans of gasoline between the two four-wheelers. They quickly transferred their gear from the Ranchero and discarded the dead men's personal effects.

"Ready?" Bolan asked Azmeh when they were settled in the Niva.

The smaller man nodded, then asked Bolan, "Do you ever weary of it?"

"What?"

"The killing."

Bolan didn't have to think about his answer. "Weary or not, it's part of the job."

The traitor was surprised when no one searched him, then thanked Allah for his luck. The Liberator pepperbox felt bulky in the waistband of his trousers, but his shirt hung loosely, and the soldiers did not notice as he climbed into the truck behind the younger of the two Americans. The gun pressed hard into his spine as he sat back against the wooden slats along the side of the truck bed, but he could live with that.

What he *could not* allow was being driven out of contact with the reinforcements he had been expecting. That would ruin everything—and, if not corrected, it would guarantee his death.

The traitor was prepared to die, if necessary, for his cause, but he preferred to delay that end. Thankfully, he had another option close at hand.

When he'd received his briefing, his superiors anticipated that the diplomats might not remain with their aircraft once it had been shot down. For that reason, to make them trackable, the traitor had been given a tiny homing beacon of his own, for use in the event that he and his companions left the plane in search of help.

The locator was built into his watch, a Timex Easy Reader, small and cheap enough that it should not lure thieves. The traitor turned it on by pressing on the stem, holding it down for three full seconds, then releasing it. The homer made no sound, of course. He simply had to trust that it was working and that his friends would track him down before it was too late.

And if they did not come? His backup orders were the same. Take out as many of the diplomats as possible, at whatever cost.

The Niva handled well. Knobby off-road tires and heavy-duty shocks smoothed out the ride that had been getting rocky in the old Ranchero. Now they could make up for lost time.

"We have a second beacon signal," Azmeh told him, peering at the GPS.

"How's that?"

"A second signal," Bolan's guide repeated. "It's moving north while the other one stays in place."

"The reader's not malfunctioning?"

Azmeh examined it more closely. "Not that I can see," he said, a moment later.

Bolan thought it through. First, it was clear the aircraft couldn't move, unless someone had shown up with a crane and flatbed truck to salvage it. That was beyond the realm of plausibility, so he discarded the idea.

More likely: the lost flight's passengers were on the move, including someone fitted with a homing beacon. Why abandon their best hope of being found, unless they had been threatened somehow? Why go north instead of east, toward Iraq? How many might be on the move?

Bolan could answer none of those questions until he'd reached the plane and checked it out. He considered changing course but let it go. It would be irresponsible to strike off in a new direction until he knew the score.

"What shall we do?" asked Azmeh.

"Head on to the plane," Bolan replied. "If no one's there, we'll track the second beacon."

"And what if the party has scattered?"

"We'll pick up whoever we can, find out why the others took off, then decide."

Azmeh nodded. "What if someone arrived ahead of us and took all of them?"

It was the rock-bottom, worst-case scenario.

"Could be," Bolan acknowledged. "If we find nobody at the crash site, we still have the second beacon. We'll run it down and see what's happening."

If the UN group had been collected by a search party, Bolan would have to see which side had beat him to the plane—and whether they'd left anyone alive. Supporters of the regime might be hostile to the interlopers, might even decide to bury them and make the problem go away. If they'd been found by rebels, on the other hand...

He couldn't finish that thought. From what Bolan knew of opposition to the Syrian regime, it was disjointed, with as much infighting as you might find at a drunken family reunion. The diplomat Muhammad Qabbani was closest to the Free Syrian Army wing, which could place him at odds with the Islamic Front, the Ahfad al-Rasul Brigade or other factions itching for a chance to wound the FSA.

Regardless, Bolan was charged with finding six men, protecting them if he could—and failing that, making sure they did no lasting harm.

The game, he understood, could still go either way.

NASSER AL-KASSAR WAS glum and silent, staring through sunglasses at the endless sprawl of desert all around him. Sergeant Zureiq pushed the UAZ-469 staff car to its limit, shimmying and lurching, but al-Kassar still wished for greater speed to overtake his enemies and claim the crash survivors for himself.

His mission—very possibly his life—depended on it.

It had started as a simple plan: the plane would be shot down, and anyone who managed to survive the crash would be collected by al-Kassar's team from the FSA. They would be executed, with the shooting videotaped for broadcast worldwide, placing blame on the Syrian army and, by extension, the entire regime.

Al-Kassar was riding in a vehicle appropriated from the army, trailed by a stolen BTR-40 and a Ural-375D utility truck, also liberated from the enemy. He and his men wore regular Syrian army fatigues with the proper insignia. On tape, they would appear legitimate, and the denials from Damascus would ring hollow after so many lies about chemical weapons and the slaughter of unarmed civilians.

It was perfect—until he lost the targets.

Now al-Kassar was playing catch-up, knowing he would likely have to fight a hostile force equal to or larger than his own. There was a world of difference between engaging army regulars and lining up a group of helpless captives for elimination.

Still, he thought they had a decent chance. He had two SGM medium machine guns chambered in 7.62×54 mm R, each capable of firing seven hundred rounds per minute. His twenty-five infantrymen, all battle-tested veterans, carried AK-47 assault rifles or the lighter AKS-74U carbines.

Al-Kassar guessed that when—not if—he overtook his enemies, the fighting would be brisk, up close and personal. The interloping diplomats he had been sent to find and execute might go down in the cross fire, but that posed no problem for al-Kassar. Alive or dead, they served him. Corpses could be passed off as victims of a firing squad. Al-Kassar could strut and pose in front of them, letting the camera linger on his badges and insignia of rank.

The plan *would* work, if he could pull it off.

Another hour, maybe ninety minutes, and the sun would set. Al-Kassar might have to stop and camp, as nightfall hid the faint trail of his foes and made his convoy's headlights visible for miles. Announcing his approach was suicide, and driving in the desert without lights was not much better.

Al-Kassar preferred surprise if it was feasible—but not if it included crashing into a wadi and breaking his neck, or driving into a bloody ambush.

When the time came, the advantage would be his.

"Where do you think they're taking us?" Dale Walton muttered.

Segrest considered it and answered quietly, "To

someone in authority. Their top man is a captain, three stars on his shoulders, so I'm guessing that we're on our way to meet a major or a colonel, maybe a brigadier general."

Walton frowned. "Can't say I like the sound of that."

"It beats a bullet in the head back at the crash site. I'm thinking our disposal is above this captain's pay grade."

"*Disposal*? Are you serious?"

"Hey, we knew what we were getting into, right? A flight to Syria, no clearance from the president, prime minister, the military—we were briefed on this, remember? It was meant to be a covert mission."

"No one mentioned being shot out of the sky," Walton complained.

"We all lived through it," Segrest said, then caught himself. "Well, not the crew, God rest their souls."

The words sounded hollow, even to him.

"So, how do we get out of this?"

"We don't. It's down to State now, and the White House. There'll be protests from Damascus, possibly denials out of Washington and the UN, to start."

Dale gaped at him. "You're saying they might cut us loose?"

"Relax. You know the drill. There's a procedure to be followed in negotiating our release. Face-saving's necessary on both sides. It could take time."

"Take time?" Dale echoed. "I've got an anniversary next month. Two years."

"We'll probably be home by then," Segrest replied. "If not, Marcie will understand. She's got a good head on her shoulders."

"I don't know about you," said Walton, "but I haven't been receiving hazard pay."

"Imagine the reception when we get back home. Party time at Foggy Bottom."

"Yeah, I guess," Walton allowed.

Unless they hang us out to dry—or me, specifically, Segrest thought. It wasn't his fault that they'd been shot down, but just like with any other bureaucracy, shit tended to roll downhill at the State Department. Someone was always to blame for snafus. In a case like this, Segrest could be the sacrificial goat.

And if he was, so what? He'd put in fifteen years at State, served two administrations. He had a Ph.D. and law license to fall back on, and he was still young enough to stake a claim for himself in the corporate world or academia. Maybe he'd write a book about the bungled jaunt to Syria and do some profitable finger-pointing of his own.

Assuming that he made it home alive.

"You don't think they'll lock us up, do you?" Dale asked. "Or…or *execute* us?"

"Cool it, will you?" Segrest said. "When was the last time anybody executed diplomats? We've got immunity."

"You heard the captain. Sneaking into Syria, we're *spies*. They might—"

"Before you piss yourself, *relax*. Sit back and take a breath. Anything they do will be in public, for the photo ops and sound bytes. They've been trying to avoid a US military intervention for the past three years. They won't be executing anybody."

Well, he thought, maybe Qabbani and his sidekick.

They were probably fair game, but two Americans and a head honcho out of UN headquarters? Not even close.

Now, if Segrest could only make himself believe that, he'd be fine.

Syrian Arab Army Headquarters, Damascus

BRIGADIER GENERAL FIRAS MOURAD was preparing to leave for the day when he heard the beep of his satphone in his desk. He doubled back from the office doorway, unlocked the drawer and lifted the phone to his ear.

"Yes?"

"Good evening, General Mourad."

He recognized the voice, of course. Few people had this number, and no stranger had ever dialed it by accident.

"Captain," Mourad said. "Do you have something to report?"

"Yes, sir. The packages have been collected."

"Ah. How many?"

"Six, sir. All in good condition."

"And you are proceeding as agreed?"

"According to your order, sir."

It was the first good news Mourad had heard today. Elsewhere in Syria, rebels had ambushed and annihilated a patrol outside Al Hasakah, while car bombs had wreaked havoc in Aleppo and Palmyra. Furious, the president himself had raged at the army's chief of staff, who had then raged against his marshals, who had passed it on down the chain of command.

"This pleases me," Mourad allowed, the strongest approbation he would offer to a subordinate. Why should

his underlings be praised extravagantly for perform-
ing as expected?

"Thank you, sir!"

Ignoring him, he asked, "You camp with them tonight?"

"Yes, sir. They are secure."

"I hope so, Captain. For your sake."

"Yes, sir. And in the morning, are we still proceeding to Damascus?"

"No. The plan has changed. I will be joining you at
your location for the court-martial. A film crew will
accompany me."

"You shall be welcome, sir!" the captain gushed.

"It's not a social meeting," Mourad answered. "We
will carry on as planned, besides the change of scene."

Chastened, the captain said, "Yes, sir! All shall be
ready for you on arrival."

"If there's nothing else, then?"

"No, sir."

Mourad cut the link.

He had decided, after all, that it would not be wise
to try the captives in Damascus. His superiors might
attempt to intervene, and through their meddling, hand
a gift to the persistent opposition. No, he would conduct
the trial himself, pass judgment on the interlopers and
observe their execution as spies. The whole proceeding would be filmed, that record locked away until such
time as Mourad needed it for his own purposes.

As for the UN flight, it would come down to a simple
disappearance. Even if nomads found the plane, the fate
of those it carried would remain a mystery. No one from
the United States or the UN could complain about the
disappearance of a secret group invading Syria with the

intent of toppling its elected government. And if they *did* complain, against all reason, then and only then would General Mourad reveal his evidence to shame them in the world's eyes, as they so richly deserved.

And in the meantime, further "diplomatic" forays into Syria would be discouraged by the fate of those who went before.

It was a good plan, he believed. He would sleep well tonight, before an early liftoff for the desert east of Deir ez-Zor.

Deir ez-Zor Governorate

THE TRAITOR ATE THE tabbouleh he had been served. He normally enjoyed the dish, but tonight he barely tasted it, chewing distractedly and pondering the next step he should take.

It was too late to kill his fellow passengers; that much was clear. At least, he could not do it in the way originally envisioned. He had no idea, now, whether his comrades were pursuing him with plans to carry out their mission, or if he had been abandoned to his fate.

The Liberator pepperbox was useless to him now. Four rounds against the twenty soldiers who had captured him and his companions from the aircraft had been a hopeless proposition, even more so when he had found another twenty waiting for them at the desert campsite where they meant to pass the night. The pistol still might help him seize a better weapon—one of the Kalashnikovs, perhaps, or better still, one of the NSV heavy machine guns mounted atop their armored personnel carriers.

He knew that surviving such a last-ditch move would be nearly impossible.

But if he had to sacrifice himself, the traitor was prepared.

That suicide scenario would not fulfill his mission, obviously. It would not appear to be an army execution of the diplomats who came in search of peace for Syria, but he supposed that headquarters might find a way to spin it, so the goal would be more or less achieved.

The hope of rescue had already faded from his mind, leaving only a grim determination in its place.

"ALL GONE," BOLAN SAID.

"All but this one, and the two inside the plane," Sabah Azmeh observed.

One pilot and a crewman he supposed had been the flight attendant had evidently died in the crash. The passengers had left them as they were, unburied, probably believing that a rescue party would have means of carting off the dead. The other pilot had survived, though badly injured, until someone had put a bullet through his head.

Darkness had already settled on the crash site. Bolan and Azmeh used night-vision goggles to survey the scene, noting the tire tracks that obliterated one another, marking the passage of at least six vehicles. He couldn't say when they had reached the scene, much less who had been driving, but all signs pointed to two separate groups, one trailing the other.

"Someone took the passengers," he said. "Then someone else came through and followed them."

"Northbound," Azmeh agreed.

Bolan reviewed the map of Syria he'd memorized.

From where they stood, the nearest city was Al Hasakah, say, eighty miles due north. Beyond that, another sixty-five miles, the Turkish border would be guarded and patrolled. Without knowing who'd grabbed the diplomats, he found it difficult—make that impossible—to guess what they'd do next.

Bolan had nothing but tracks to guide him. He could only follow, hoping that he overtook the prisoners before it was too late.

He turned back to the Niva SUV, boots crunching on the hardpan. Azmeh followed and climbed into the shotgun seat.

Bolan kept the goggles on and the Niva's headlights off as he drove, scanning the night for fire, taillights, anything at all that might direct him, but so far, the darkness was complete.

No, wait. There *was* a light, away to Bolan's left, sweeping across the desert. Well above it, four hundred feet or so, he saw two smaller, blinking lights, one red and one green.

Bolan knew a helicopter when he saw one, even when he couldn't make out any details of its size or shape. Out here, airborne patrols meant army or air force, and the choppers would be Russian, either the Mil Mi-24 Hind, or its little brother, the Mil Mi-2 Hoplite. Both carried 57 mm rockets and 23 mm cannons, and the Hind also had a heavy machine gun in its chin turret.

Either way, bad news for targets on the ground.

"They see us," Azmeh said, whispering as if the soldiers in the helicopter could hear them, too.

And he was right. Bolan saw the searchlight sweeping toward them. The Niva's headlights had been off, but infrared technology onboard would have easily picked up the vehicle, drawing the helicopter to them like a porch lamp draws insects.

"Can you reach the RPG behind me?" he asked Azmeh.

"Yes."

"Bring it up front, then. And hang on," he cautioned. "This is where the ride gets bumpy."

By the time Azmeh had pulled the rocket launcher forward, their airborne pursuer had cut the distance between them in half.

"Bail out on my signal," he told Azmeh. "Don't stay near the car if you can help it."

If the Arab answered, Bolan didn't catch it. He was focused on the spotlight racing toward them, ticking off split seconds in his head before he made his move.

8

Washington, DC

Hal Brognola was eating lunch at his desk when the White House line demanded his attention, the red light winking on his telephone's base unit. Six lines coming in, and this one always made his stomach churn.

Brognola set his sandwich down and lifted the receiver to his ear. "Brognola."

"Hal, Vic Tomlinson."

Officially, Deputy Assistant to the President and Principal Deputy Counsel to the President, a two-headed title that let him maul subordinates with two sarcastic mouths.

"What can I do for you?"

"We were hoping for an update on this thing in Syria. Some good news, preferably."

"You'll hear as soon as I do."

"Hal, we have a couple of old men up on the Hill who think it's time for SEALs to take their shot."

"Not something I'd suggest."

"No, of course not. But we need *results*, Hal. *Positive* results. I'm not clear on the reason why we're handling this through Justice in the first place—"

And you never will be, Brognola thought.

"—but unless we see some action *soon*, I'll have to recommend another avenue. I know that stings, but it's a fact of life."

"I'm used to stings, Vic. At this point, redundant efforts would be self-defeating."

"Meaning what?"

"Exactly what I said."

"It might help if I knew what you were doing, Hal."

"I'm sure your boss has told you everything he feels you need to know."

He could feel Tomlinson simmering, pictured his sour face behind the grand desk in his West Wing office.

"Hal, in case there's any doubt about who calls the shots here—"

"None at all. I'm entirely clear on that."

It certainly wasn't Tomlinson.

Only the President was fully briefed on Stony Man, its background and its mission. His subordinates occasionally got an order—"Talk to Hal Brognola, see what he says"—and the world moved on without them micromanaging events. Some liked it that way, others didn't. Vic Tomlinson was a man with an inflated sense of self-importance who could make life miserable in the short term until someone yanked his leash.

Tomlinson got the message. That he didn't like it was a given, but the worst that he could do was bluster.

"Hal, I have to tell you, this is on a ticking clock."

"Yes, I understand the urgency."

"Jobs may depend on it."

"And lives," Brognola added.

"Right. Of course, that has to be our first consideration."

"Always has and always will be."

"I hope so. And I hope that I'll be hearing from you soon."

"A hope I share, Mr. Tomlinson."

The line went dead, with no goodbye.

Deir ez-Zor Governorate, Syria

BOLAN LEAPED FROM the Niva as soon as he switched off its motor, carrying the RPG-7. The SUV's dome lights were out, maybe something its late former owners had rigged for convenience, and he left the driver's door wide open. Behind him, he heard Sabah Azmeh jump out and make a run for it, as instructed.

Not that it would help, if the advancing chopper's searchlight fell on either one of them.

The Hind and Hoplite helicopters varied in more than size, weight and armament, but neither one would shrug off a direct hit from one of Bolan's 93 mm rocket-propelled HEAT warheads.

Bottom line: Bolan could bring down either model—if he hit it.

Bolan would have to do it right the first time out. He hadn't grabbed a second rocket from the Niva's backseat, and he likely wouldn't have time to reload the launcher anyway, if his first warhead missed its mark.

The searchlight found his ride, swept to the pilot's right, and froze on Bolan.

He recognized the stutter of a heavy machine gun and saw its muzzle-flashes winking at him from the helicopter's chin. That meant he had a Hind to deal with and would have to make a clean hit with his HEAT round when he let it fly.

First, though, Bolan had to dodge the storm of bullets streaming toward him. He hit the ground and rolled, took a beating on his shoulder from the launcher's tube, and came up in a crouch, squinting through its sight into the searchlight's blinding glare.

"THEY'RE RUNNING FOR IT," said Captain Duraid Shaladi.

"I see that," Captain Farid Nasny replied tersely. He was the Hind's lead pilot and, as such, had perfect eyesight.

"Look, they're armed!" Shaladi blurted.

"Again, I see them," Nasny answered. Then, to his chin turret gunner, "Engage targets, Sergeant Atiyeh."

"Yes, sir!" came the shooter's voice, tinny and small through his earpiece.

The turret piece was an NSV heavy machine gun, which mangled men and vehicles with equal proficiency, leaving death and ruin in its wake. And if the NSV failed, Captain Nasny still had his twin-barreled GSh-23 autocannon, capable of spewing 23x115 mm rounds at a rate of up to 3,600 per minute. If *that* failed to finish off his target, he had a pod of four 9M114 *Kokon* radio-guided antitank missiles on standby for heavier work.

Unfortunately, even with so much firepower on tap, pinning down a single runner—or two men who had separated—could be difficult. The NSV's rounds were devastating to flesh and bone on impact, but they flew where the gunner aimed them, and if the man in his sights was unpredictable and agile, shredding him could take some time.

And time meant ammunition.

"Reloading, Captain!" Atiyeh advised.

Cursing, Captain Nasny readied his GSh-23 cannon. The weapon fed its rotating barrels from two cylindrical drums, each holding 200 rounds. Given the cannon's higher rate of fire, both drums could be empty within seconds if Nasny got trigger-happy, but his helmet/sight interface assisted in aiming.

Sadly, it did nothing to slow down his bobbing, weaving human targets.

One of them was firing at the helicopter with an automatic rifle now—pathetic, since its bullets could not penetrate the cockpit, fuselage or rotor blades. The other target worried Nasny, though. He carried what appeared to be a rocket launcher, its bulky warhead telling him it had to be an RPG-7. This was trouble. If the runner knew what he was doing, and Nasny gave him a chance to aim his weapon properly, he could cripple the Hind and send it hurtling to Earth.

Still, there could be no turning back. He had target acquisition, and the enemy had been engaged. To break off contact in the middle of a firefight was unthinkable, humiliating. How could he go home and tell his colonel they had spotted two guerrillas in the desert and allowed them to escape?

He could fall back and blast their vehicle, but that seemed cowardly when Nasny had the speed, maneuverability and firepower on his side. The contest should be his.

"Look out!" Sharadi shouted, too late, as the RPG's backflash lit up the ground below.

Nasny watched the rocket sail toward his helicopter on a tail of flame.

SABAH AZMEH TRIPPED over a stone and fell facedown, skinning his palms on gravel as his momentum carried him another six or seven feet. He'd done his part at the beginning, jumping from the SUV on Cooper's order, ducking to avoid the searchlight's sweeping beam, then firing at the helicopter with his AKMS as the aircraft roared above him, blotting out the stars with its insectile bulk.

And then, Allah forgive him, he had tried to run away.

It was impossible, he realized. Fleeing from airborne hunters in this wasteland was futile. He had nowhere to hide, no sane hope of outrunning his assailants.

Falling like a clumsy child had saved him this time, but he was about to die; he was sure of it. The helicopter roared past, spitting rounds from its chin turret, raising foot-tall spurts of dust that drifted over Azmeh's prostrate form, filling one eye with grit.

As it passed, he struggled to his feet once more and chose a new direction—east instead of south—hoping he might confuse the pilots and machine-gunner just long enough for them to miss him on their next pass. Long enough, perhaps, for Cooper to have a chance with his RPG.

Or was he dead already?

It was possible, and what would Azmeh do then? Spend the last chaotic moments of his life trying to dodge a rain of mangling bullets from the sky.

No, he decided. At the very least, he could stand up and face death like a man, rather than cowering and fleeing like a rodent.

In the other fights with Cooper, Azmeh had been startled by his own sense of exhilaration. There was fear, of course, but he had been elated that, at last, he was *doing* something. Azmeh could not guess what might result from following the tall American, but after years of watching from the sidelines while his homeland tore itself apart, at least he was engaged. He was participating, fighting for a cause he felt was just.

But this battle was different. The other fights, with men on foot, made sense. Tonight, the killers in the Hind were hunting him, reducing him to the level of a frightened animal. His bullets could not penetrate the aircraft's armored hide, but he could still distract its crew, perhaps, and sell his life for a purpose, rather than just throwing it away.

Azmeh stopped short and turned back to face the gunship on the last pass it would need to kill him. Another stone slipped underneath his left heel, making him stagger and nearly fall as the machine-gunner unleashed another spray of bullets.

One passed through the narrow space between Azmeh's left arm and side, scorching his flesh and flaying the skin above his ribs. The impact knocked him aside as if he were a clump of windblown chaff. This time, he landed on his back, huffing the last air from his lungs as he connected with the hardpan.

Still alive, he thought through the scalding pain, and groped around for the carbine he had dropped when he went down.

CAPTAIN NASNY TRIED TO avoid the rocket as it soared to meet him, seeming to be aimed directly at his face. He angled the chopper upward, seeking altitude, accelerating as he climbed, then swung away northward, hopefully letting the rocket pass by him with inches to spare. Knowing the aircraft as he did, Nasny surmised that he could circle once around and spray the earth-bound shooter with his autocannon, turning him into shredded meat before the man could reload the RPG.

It almost worked.

Nasny *did* save himself from a direct hit on the Hind's cockpit, but there was no time for him to outrun, much less outmaneuver, the warhead hurtling toward his aircraft.

The rocket connected where the fuselage became the helicopter's tail, a narrowing behind the stubby left-hand wing where fuel lines ran beside critical cables and wiring to keep the bird airborne. All of that was blasted into ruins now, the tail sheared off and falling free, while Nasny tried to compensate with the controls.

No use.

The Hind was going down. The best that he could hope for was a "safe" crash landing, sparing him and his two crewmen any major injury. The ship still had its landing gear, as far as he could tell, but when Nasny attempted to deploy the wheels he set off fresh alarms, competing with the ones already blaring through his headset.

"Fuck!" he raged into his mouthpiece, unaware if anyone could hear him.

Nasny had been trained in belly landings, for emergencies, and this was bound to qualify. The risk involved in coming down that way was ruptured fuel tanks, splashing gasoline around the wounded aircraft's hot machinery and sparking wires. The Hind might well explode, and if it did, he would be cooked alive with his companions.

But he had no choice. The bird was coming down, with or without Nasny at the controls. It spun above the desert floor, a smoking whirlwind, swiftly losing altitude. He needed both hands for the controls, no time for the radio, but hoped Shaladi might be sending a distress signal.

On impact, Nasny felt as if his spine had shattered. Smoke and dust surrounded him, obscuring the moonlit landscape as he grappled with his safety harness, barking out his crewmen's names. "Duraid! Ahed!"

Both answered weekly, sounding dazed. Nasny finally got his harness off and turned to wriggle from his seat, struggling toward freedom in the moments left before a spark met fuel and turned the shattered Hind into a blazing pyre. He stepped on someone in the scramble, barely heard the bitter curse, and moved on toward the exit.

When he cleared the hatch, Nasny sucked in a deep lungful of smoke that gagged him and left him retching as he tumbled out. It was his turn to be stepped on now, as someone else dropped from the hatch, soon followed by a third person, who fell across his legs.

All present and accounted for, but still not safe.

"With me!" he croaked, and started crawling farther from the wreckage on all fours.

ALL THAT REMAINED was the cleanup. The rocket strike had been a combination of skill and luck, and now

Bolan had to deal with any survivors who had managed to escape the dying Hind.

The Russian chopper was already burning, flames licking around the section where its tail was torn away. The fuel tanks would explode any moment now.

Bolan walked wide around the wreckage, looking for Sabah Azmeh, and found him coming back toward the Niva, holding his left arm a little apart from his torso. His shirt on that side was darkly stained.

"Are you hit?" Bolan asked him.

"A graze, I believe."

"We'll check it as soon as I finish up here."

"Let me help you."

"No, thanks. Have a seat in the truck and relax."

Three men had managed to escape the Hind after it crashed. He found them on the east side of the wreckage, clearly visible by firelight. He might have told their ranks from the insignia they wore, but that was insignificant. Allowing even one to crawl away could be the death of him, Azmeh and the men they'd come to rescue from Syria.

The nearest enemy saw Bolan coming and pushed up to a kneeling posture as he tried to reach a semiauto pistol in a standard pilot's shoulder holster. Bolan drilled his forehead with a single bullet and the guy flopped over with his legs folded beneath him.

His shot put the remaining airmen on alert. One, crawling away from the wreck and dragging a broken leg behind him, fumbled for a pistol in a rig just like his crewmate's. The guy had managed to unstrap it and was drawing his weapon when a round from Bolan's AKMS smashed into his face.

The final member of the chopper's crew was on his

feet, his pistol drawn. Bolan didn't feel like playing *High Noon* with the guy, so he cut off the showdown with a double-tap to center mass that pulped his heart and left him dying on his feet. The pistol tumbled from dead fingers, and the crewman folded like an empty suit of clothes, its hanger snatched away.

Now Bolan had to check on Azmeh and the SUV, make sure that both were fit for travel, and he could resume the desert chase.

9

Damascus International Airport

Brigadier General Firas Mourad had decided not to wait for sunrise, after all. He would surprise Captain Fakhri, arriving early, and they would conduct the court-martial around midnight, which seemed appropriate.

The hour of judgment, when grim deeds were sheltered by darkness.

Mourad was flying in a Mil Mi-8 helicopter, with seating for twenty-four passengers. His party was only one-fourth that size, including himself, his personal aide Major Raed Farzat, three cameramen and Captain Samer Khalil, who fancied himself a film director.

The court-martial was not precisely scripted, but Mourad and Captain Khalil had made notes in advance, considered preparation for reactions from the prisoners, and even sketched the final scene that was the purpose of the whole grim exercise. There was an art to execution, most particularly when a group of six stood up before a firing squad. Mourad was making *history*, and since he planned to capture it on film, he wanted the result to be *historic*.

If the world was never given the privilege of viewing his work, so be it. He would file the tapes away until such time as the United Nations or the US State Department voiced concern over their missing "diplomats." At that time, once they had effectively confessed to their conspiracy against the Syrian Arab Republic, Mourad would unveil proof positive of their illegal actions, including their agents' confessions of guilt.

Voilà!

The world at large would be amazed, his country's enemies humiliated in the spotlight of aggrieved public opinion. Following the years of meddling, sanctions and killer drone attacks, Syria would be cast in sympathetic light for once.

The helicopter lifted off at 9:15 p.m. Even flying at a modest one hundred sixty miles per hour, he expected to reach Captain Fakhri's desert camp by 10:45, plenty of time to set the stage and brief his players on their roles. Mourad expected some resistance from the villains of the piece, which would be only natural, but there were ways of overcoming that initial reticence that left no visible signs of abuse. When the cameras rolled at last, every member of the cast would know his part and would perform on cue.

Or else.

Mourad had a trick up his sleeve, for starters. He would promise the prisoners freedom if they accommodated his needs. Simply confess to entering Syria without permission and with devious intent—a crime of which they were, in fact, guilty—and they regained their freedom. What could be more generous, under the circumstances?

Well satisfied with his decision and arrangements, Mourad settled back and closed his eyes.

He had a long night still ahead of him and planned to look his very best before the cameras.

Deir ez-Zor Governorate

"WHAT DO YOU THINK we're waiting for?" Dale Walton whispered.

Beside him, Roger Segrest shrugged. "Beats me. I thought they would've let us go to sleep by now."

Or put us all to sleep, he thought.

The possibility of death had been on Segrest's mind since the soldiers showed up at the crash site. Scratch that—since the plane fell out of the sky. There was no doubt that they'd be charged with spying and some variation of subversion, both of which were capital offenses at the moment, under martial law. Hanging, he'd been told, was the lawful means of execution, but he also knew that certain military units made exceptions in the field, without a gallows handy.

Any way you sliced it, dead was dead.

"It looks like they're expecting someone," Walton said, keeping an eye out for the guard who had forbidden conversation between prisoners.

"Some higher-up," Segrest replied, lips barely moving. "Maybe someone from the Ministry of Defense."

Of course, he might be flattering himself. Upon his arrest, Segrest had identified himself, giving his name, rank and serial number. As the third-highest ranking US official to visit Syria since the civil war began, his name would mean something. Not to the captain who had captured them, perhaps, but to his superiors at headquarters. The same held true with Sani Bankole, a rising star at UN headquarters.

"We can't just disappear," said Walton.

And the devil's advocate in Segrest's head replied, why not?

Officially, they weren't in Syria. Bankole's party and his own were booked into the Al Rasheed Hotel in Baghdad for a weeklong conference on issues that included Syria, along with the ongoing turmoil in Iraq and nuclear negotiations with Iran. Their whole itinerary had been printed in advance, supported by a list of shadowy witnesses at the hotel. Who was to say they could not simply disappear?

There'd be a major stink, of course. Four diplomats—Qabbani and his sidekick didn't count; they weren't on record as being involved in the proceedings—couldn't simply drop off the face of the earth without some ripples spreading. At some point, possibly next week, four anxious families would hear a suitably redacted version of events. A plane crash in the desert, possibly, with searches underway. If commercial jets with hundreds of passengers could vanish on routine flights, why not a small aircraft with nine aboard, somewhere in the troubled Middle East?

The flip side of that coin was the publicity Syria's regime could get by parading enemy agents across the world stage. The president could strike a martyr's pose, perhaps gain sympathy in quarters where he had been losing friends. And Moscow, doubtless, would be pleased by the embarrassment to Washington.

However it played out—whether he wound up being

executed, jailed or sent home in disgrace—Segrest supposed the rocket that had downed their plane had also finished his career at State. No one could publicly accuse him of a screwup, but he could forget about promotion, and he'd likely be encouraged to resign.

"Whatever happens," he told Walton, "keep in mind the nature of our mission. It's above top secret. You acknowledge nothing, ever."

"Understood." His aide looked doubly worried now, causing Segrest to feel a fleeting pang of guilt.

"But, hey—don't worry. They'll most likely hold a press conference, rip Uncle Sam a new one and send us packing."

"I hope so," Walton said.

Segrest studied the soldiers who surrounded them and thought, I hope so, too.

Compared to the alternatives, a premature retirement sounded pretty sweet.

BOLAN PATCHED THE wounds on Azmeh's side and left biceps. His guide's assessment had been right; the bullet had just grazed him. While he cleaned and dressed the injuries, Bolan was conscious of the time. He couldn't know if anyone aboard the Hind had called in to report contact with enemies or sent off a Mayday signal as they dropped out of the sky, and he'd prefer to be on the move again before another chopper showed up on the scene. As far as Bolan knew, the opposition fighters had nothing in the way of aircraft, meaning that the helicopter he'd shot down was army or air force.

He had joined battle with the government, although they didn't know it yet.

The second beacon they had followed from the crash

site wasn't moving. There were several explanations for that: the missing passengers might have camped for the night with whoever retrieved them, or they could have been forced to change clothes and discard their belongings.

Worst-case scenario, they could be dead now, waiting for the jackals and hyenas to arrive.

"Do you think we'll find them?" Azmeh asked as Bolan secured the last of his bandages.

"We'll keep trying," Bolan said.

"And if the army has them? Then, what?"

"Then you've got another call to make," Bolan replied. "Whether you want to see it through or take a pass."

"I am no friend of the regime," Azmeh said.

"No. But if the odds get any worse…"

"We made a deal. I stay until the end, whatever that may be."

Bolan nodded and shook his guide's hand. "Deal." He checked the GPS again. "We've got about another seventy miles."

Unless somebody else got in their way.

CAPTAIN NASSER AL-KASSAR frowned at the GPS device and shook it lightly, as if that would move him closer to his goal. Their progress, if he chose to call it that, seemed maddeningly slow, despite the fact that they were clearly gaining ground.

"Still twenty miles," he told Aziz Zureiq.

"Another hour, at our present speed," the sergeant answered.

"Is there no way to drive faster?"

"Certainly," Zureiq replied. "At greater risk."

Al-Kassar knew that his driver was correct. They would reach the target a few minutes before eleven, more or less, if they were not diverted by a wadi or some other obstacle along the way, such as the damned nomads they had encountered some miles back. Not bad, but he was anxious to be done with this assignment after two wasted days. Already, his superiors were restless, carping at him about failure to perform. If he delayed much longer...

Zureiq interrupted his train of thought. "Do we have a plan, Captain?"

"Of course," al-Kassar replied. A poorly formed one, at least. "If the invaders have been taken by government troops, we attack and seize them."

That crude course of action assumed that they were not badly outnumbered by the enemy. In any case, al-Kassar knew he must proceed to carry out his mission. He could not tuck tail and run away, when he had come this close to resolving the matter.

"And if they were not picked up by regulars?" Zureiq pressed him.

It was a possibility, of course. With close to fifty groups battling the regime, there was a chance, however small, that some of al-Kassar's putative allies might have found the plane's crash site by accident and recognized an opportunity to ransom hostages. In theory, al-Kassar was not supposed to fight with any of the other rebel groups, but he was not about to let some gaggle from al-Qaeda or the Muslim Brotherhood rob him of victory and leave him in disgrace.

"Whoever has them," he told Zureiq, "they are ours."

The sergeant said no more, apparently content to drive and think about his own role in the battle yet to come. And there would be a battle. He had no doubt of that. Unless whoever had retrieved the interlopers gave them up without a fight, he had no choice but to take them forcibly.

That course suggested problems of its own. In order to fulfill his orders, posing as an army unit when he executed the invaders, he required sufficient men and military vehicles to make the filming realistic. Losses from whatever action he engaged in at his destination jeopardized that plan. Unless…

If they *were* facing army regulars when they arrived on target, that could work to his advantage. That meant other vehicles for stage dressing, other equipment he could use to set the stage. He would have to kill the soldiers loyal to the president, but once they were disposed of, he could use their APCs, their trucks, whatever still remained, as he saw fit.

And suddenly, al-Kassar experienced a flash of brilliance.

What if any regulars he killed were actually rebels from the FSA, slain as they tried to help the outside agitators infiltrate his country? It was just a small revision in the script, for realism's sake, and to support the motive of his faux soldiers in executing those they'd captured. Afterward, in daylight, they would backtrack to the UN plane and film it as well, to amplify the world's outrage.

Mission accomplished.

Now, he just had to pull it off.

THE TRAITOR FEIGNED sleep after an exhausting day, watching his guards through slitted eyelids. The one nearest to him seemed drowsy, yawning frequently. The next one was twenty feet away and had his back turned toward the prisoners, intent on scouring the desert night beyond the campfire's light.

The captives had been taken to a crude trench after their evening meal, where they relieved themselves under the guns and watchful eyes of soldiers. The traitor had not been intimidated by that scrutiny, but he had worried that the Liberator pepperbox might fall out of his trousers in the process, exposing him. Thankfully, he had avoided any such calamity and still retained the weapon. He was constantly aware of it, and of the minutes slipping through his hands.

It now seemed that he could not count on any outside help. Surely, if comrades from the FSA were coming, they would have arrived by now. The only thing postponing action was his own procrastination and the state of readiness he noted in the soldiers ranged around him.

It was nearly ten o'clock, and in another hour, maybe two, the guards would be more weary, more relaxed, despite their orders to remain alert. In his experience, strict discipline could only go so far toward overcoming human nature and fatigue.

The traitor craved refuge in sleep himself. Ironically, the longer he faked it, the closer he came to dozing off, and he could not afford such a lapse. To wake at dawn, with the whole camp stirring, would spoil any chance he had for the day. By tomorrow at dusk they could be in Damascus or some other city, where he would be thoroughly searched and disarmed before he was clapped in a cell.

No. He must make his move tonight, sooner rather than later. If he could remain awake until midnight...

Shifting positions slightly, silently, the traitor slipped

his right hand underneath the left arm he was using for a pillow, found the soft flesh there, and gave himself a vicious pinch, grinding his thumb and forefinger together while his teeth clenched in reaction to the sudden pain. At once, the mist cleared from his brain, and he was wide awake.

Not so, the nearest guard. His head was drooping now, as he slouched back against the fender of a truck. A few more moments, and—

"Attention!"

Instantly, the guard snapped upright, fumbling for a second with his AK-47, clicking his boot heels as he stood ramrod-straight before the sergeant of the guard. The sentry shed all signs of drowsiness and now looked embarrassed, even frightened, as he was discovered nearly sleeping at his post.

"No problems here?" the glaring sergeant asked him.

"No, sir!"

"All prisoners accounted for?"

"Yes, sir!"

"You still have two hours on duty. Do you need some coffee?"

"Yes, sir, if you have—"

"Go fetch it for yourself!" the sergeant snapped. "I'll wait exactly two minutes, then put you on report."

"Yes, sir!"

The soldier ran off toward the campfire, every step he took pumping adrenaline into his system, driving out the fog of sleep. He would remain alert over the next two hours, certainly, then be replaced by someone fresh to finish out the night.

The traitor made up his mind. He would wait a little longer, once the sergeant left, then seize the first chance he perceived to make his move. Take down the young sentry, seize his Kalashnikov—and whatever occurred from that point on was in the hands of Allah.

BOLAN WAS FORCED to slow as two camels crossed the trail illuminated by the Niva's headlights, ambling toward the Iraqi border. They were trailing leads, but neither one was packing any cargo, nor had they been saddled. Bolan watched them go, then drove another fifty yards before he saw the tattered, flattened tents ahead.

He heard Azmeh prepare his AKMS carbine. Bolan scanned the desert scene—two smallish tents, the fire burned down to smoking ashes, two more camels barely visible beyond his high beams—and quickly found the corpses. There were four of them, all clad in traditional Bedouin clothing, stained now by blood that had dried rusty brown.

Someone had come across the camp and wasted it without a second though. Whether the nomads had attempted to delay their killers or were simply in the wrong place at the wrong time, Bolan couldn't say. In either case, the end result had been the same.

He steered around the tents and corpses, picking up the faint trail he'd been following, and accelerated once he'd cleared the skirmish site. Azmeh relaxed beside him, set his carbine down, but remained vigilant.

"You think whoever took the survivors killed these guys, too?" he asked Bolan.

"Most likely, but we'll never know for sure."

That was the problem when a country turned into one massive free-fire zone. No one was safe.

"In discussions of my country," Azmeh said, after

another moment, "I hear much about the regime and the resistance, very little about common people. The outsiders who pretend to help us say democracy when they mean oil, influence, power. If the truth be told, I don't trust either side completely."

Bolan couldn't argue with his logic. He had learned enough from history to know that even in a truly just war there were villains on all sides, as well as heroes. Sometimes the end result was worse than what had gone before.

"The thing I focus on," he told Azmeh, "is getting through the job. I try to see what's wrong, right here, right now, and fix it if I can."

"Yes," Azmeh agreed. "But when you're gone, I must remain."

10

"Fifteen minutes, General," the pilot said over the helicopter's intercom.

Firas Mourad had not been sleeping, only resting with his eyes closed, but he felt refreshed as he sat up and peered out through the Mil Mi-8's small window. It was a wasted effort, nothing but dark desert below him, indistinguishable from the surface of a vast, calm sea.

He sat back, stretched his arms in front of him with fingers laced and heard crackling in his shoulder blades that told him he was getting old. Five years to go before retirement with full pension. Mourad had given up on rising to full general before he was released into civilian life, but this night's work might make the difference. If nothing else, there might be ways to profit from it personally, though he had not worked out all the details yet.

For the excursion, he had worn his "combat uniform," a euphemism for most officers of Mourad's rank, who never found themselves within a hundred miles of battle unless rebels overran their headquarters. The uniform was lizard-pattern camouflage, topped with a red beret bearing his badge of rank. The pistol on his hip, a 9×18 mm Makarov that he had never fired in anger, rode on a Sam Browne belt.

Unbuckling his safety harness, Mourad rose and tottered forward to the cockpit. Peering through its doorway, he looked over the pilot's shoulder and out through the windscreen.

The pilot noticed him and half turned to face the general. "Shall I contact the base camp, sir?"

"No contact yet," Mourad replied. "Wait until we have closed to half a mile."

"Yes, sir."

He had revised his plan to take Bassam Fakhri by complete surprise, worried that the captain's men might fire on Mourad's helicopter if he dropped in out of nowhere in the middle of the night. It would be safer this way and still produce nearly the same effect, without giving Fakhri any time to prepare for the visit.

Whenever possible, Mourad deemed it beneficial to keep his subordinates guessing, wondering what he might do or demand of them next. If they became too settled and secure, it gave them time to think, perhaps to plot against him.

The court-martial he had in mind was risky and had not been cleared by his superiors. Mourad had planned it on his own. To seek permission was to risk denial— or, worse yet, to have his plan and his success co-opted by some full-fledged general who had not spent a minute on the project after rubber-stamping Mourad's scheme. He had been relegated to the shadows more than once by higher-ranking officers, and Mourad did not plan to let it happen again.

"Five minutes, General," the pilot said. "If you'd be seated, please, and buckle up, I will alert the camp as ordered from the half-mile point."

Mourad retreated from the cockpit to his place in the front row of passenger seats. Across the aisle from him, Major Farzat appeared slightly airsick.

"We're almost there, Raed," Mourad encouraged him.

"Yes, sir."

Mourad restrained himself from laughing at the younger officer's discomfort. Here was one he never had to fear. The major's weakness was embarrassing at times, but on this night it offered reassurance to Mourad.

He was the man in charge, whatever happened next, and no one could dispute it.

"THIRTY MILES," BOLAN said after double-checking the GPS. "Your arm still holding up okay?"

"It's fine," Azmeh replied.

"Because, if you think you'll have any trouble fighting—"

"No."

"Or if you'd rather back off from this round—"

"No," he said, more emphatically. "I have not come this far to cower in the shadows."

"No one mentioned cowering."

"Same thing. *We* have work to do, not you alone."

"Okay. Just checking."

He knew damn well his guide's left arm wasn't "fine," but Azmeh had been lucky overall. They'd stopped the bleeding and forestalled infection for now.

Pain was something else entirely, though. Azmeh would simply have to live with it, fight through it.

When they reached their destination, Bolan wouldn't have the time to shelter him.

Some kind of flying creature swooped through Bolan's headlights, then disappeared into the night. "I wonder if they've begun interrogations yet," Azmeh mused.

"There's nothing we can do about it except get there as soon as possible."

"I know. But if we find some of them badly injured..."

"I'm not leaving anyone behind," Bolan informed him. "That's a given."

"Captain! A message for you, on the radio."

Bassam Fakhri rose from his camp chair, facing Sergeant Malki by firelight. "Very well," he replied. "I'm coming."

"It's too late, sir," Malki said. "I tried to keep him on the line for you, but he refused."

"'He'? Who is *he*?"

"The general, sir."

"What are you saying, Sergeant?"

"General Mourad, sir. He's arriving any minute now."

At first, Fakhri thought Malki must have lost his mind, but then he decided it was just the sort of underhanded trick Mourad might play on a subordinate. Schedule a meeting for first light, then show up hours early in the hope of catching Fakhri unprepared, perhaps with lapses in security that could be cited in a critical report.

"Wake up the men who aren't on duty," he barked

at Malki. "Have them fall in for inspection, if the general is so inclined."

"Yes, sir!" Malki ran off to do as he'd been told.

Fakhri approached the captives under guard. Most of them seemed to be asleep, or else they were faking it. He raised his voice, addressing them in English. "Everyone get up! General Firas Mourad is arriving to begin the state's investigation of your criminal offense."

The African, Bankole, was the first man on his feet. "Captain, I must protest—"

"Save any protestations for the general," Fakhri said, interrupting him. "Aside from guarding you, my role in the proceeding is concluded."

Which was not entirely true, of course. If General Mourad decided execution was appropriate for the invaders, Fakhri would carry out the order, and he would not falter. Since the onset of the civil war, he'd executed scores of rebels, spies and terrorists, sometimes without seeking advice from his superiors. The president's command was crystal-clear: no mercy would be shown to traitors, although punishment might be delayed until news cameras had left the scene.

There would be no intrusion by the media this time.

He heard a helicopter's engines now. Malki roused sleepy soldiers from their tents. Their uniforms were rumpled, some of them were yawning, but it was the best Fakhri could do on such short notice. Not even Mourad himself could turn out spit-and-polish troops in desert bivouac, with two minutes to spare.

The Mil Mi-8 touched down in a cloud of dust, its engines quieting and rotors slowing once its fat tires connected with the hardpan. Fakhri dropped the arm that he had raised to shield his eyes from flying grit, brushed dust from his fatigues, and started toward the helicopter with a fixed smile on his face. Whatever happened next, he would seem pleased to see the general and welcome him with all due courtesy.

Mourad was first out of the helicopter, trailed by Major Farzat, who was clearly struggling to keep his dinner down. Fakhri snapped to attention as Mourad approached, offering a sharp salute that was returned with some insouciance by the general.

"At ease, Captain," Mourad ordered. "Upon consideration, I decided there was no point waiting until dawn."

"No, sir. As you prefer."

"I haven't caught you sleeping?"

"No, sir. Far from it."

Mourad seemed disappointed, but it quickly passed. "All right, then. Take me to the prisoners."

THE TRAITOR RECOGNIZED Firas Mourad on sight. Each fighter in the FSA was duty bound to memorize the faces of all generals who served the Syrian regime, in case they ever came upon one of the savages and had an opportunity to strike a blow against the enemy. For most, that was an idle fantasy, but now the traitor saw fate handing him a chance to realize one of his fondest dreams.

Mourad was known for having ordered various atrocities: torture of prisoners, murder of medical personnel and their patients, massacres of whole villages whose occupants were accused of holding rebel sympathies. Next to the president and his chief of staff, Mourad was the FSA's most wanted target. Or call him *least* wanted.

As soon as he spotted Mourad, the traitor knew what

he must do. Killing the peacemakers immediately took a backseat to eliminating the general despised by every freedom-seeking Syrian. His plan could be revised without much difficulty—kill the nearest guard and seize his rifle, make it to the APC and put its heavy machine gun to work—and with only slight adjustment of the target.

But the traitor also saw his difficulty: he was clearly running out of time.

Instead of reinforcements, Mourad had brought three soldiers bearing cameras and microphones, plus two more whose duties appeared to consist of just standing around. Mourad spoke to the captain, who in turn directed soldiers to begin striking their tents, clearing a space within the camp for some event that was the focus of the exercise.

Something worth taping for posterity.

An execution, possibly, in which case the traitor could stand back and let Mourad complete his own original assignment. It would cost him his life, but if he knew that the negotiators would be killed, their deaths inevitably spiking outrage against the regime, it would be worth the sacrifice. On the other hand, missing his chance to kill Mourad would be a failure he could scarcely tolerate.

It might even prevent his passage into Paradise.

None of the hostages were feigning sleep now. Beside him, Muhammad Qabbani whispered, "Do you recognize that one?"

"General Mourad."

"And no escort to speak of."

Other than the forty soldiers already in camp, of course. The traitor cared nothing for them. It did not matter if they killed him now, as long as he had time to put at least one bullet through the general's ugly, smirking face.

Even the Liberator pepperbox might do it, if Mourad came close enough, but he preferred the thought of commandeering a machine gun, pouring automatic fire into the butcher's body, shredding him and leaving only pulp even a mother would not recognize. Whatever happened after that, the traitor knew his soul was safe.

But wait! Mourad was moving toward them now, trailing the captain and an aide who looked as if he had a seriously upset stomach. The traitor scrambled to his feet and slipped one hand behind his back, touching the blocky handle of his 3D-printed weapon.

Just a few more steps…

And then it happened. Someone on the southern edge of camp called out, "Captain Fakhri! We have vehicles coming, sir!"

Mourad and his companions stopped dead in their tracks, all frowning, and turned back the way they'd come. Fakhri was shouting orders, rallying his men to meet the new arrivals. No one seemed to know who the latecomers might be.

"Some kind of camp, I think," Sergeant Zureiq said when they were still a mile out from the main fire and its smaller satellites.

Captain al-Kassar made out electric lights, as well, though he could not tell whether they came from vehicles or floodlights. The latter made no sense. Why draw more attention to the bivouac in darkness, in an active war zone, than the fires already had?

"We'll soon find out," he told Zureiq. "Switch off your lights now."

"Yes, sir." The desert in between them and the camp went dark.

He picked up his radio, repeating the order to both of his following drivers, and saw their headlights die. It might be too late already, he knew, if the camp had guards posted. And why would it not? Still, there was a slight possibility of surprising whoever had picked this place to spend the night. With luck, it might turn out to be the party that had seized the diplomats—his rightful property—and he could solve two problems at once.

If it turned out to be more nomads, he might still collect some useful information from them, if they'd seen a convoy passing with the prisoners. If not...well, that was their hard luck.

Lifting the radio again, he warned the other vehicles, "Be ready for quick action when we stop."

He pictured his soldiers cocking their rifles, preparing the APC's heavy machine gun. Several of the AKMs had been fitted with a GP-25 Kostyor—"bonfire"—grenade launcher, capable of hurling a 40 mm caseless projectile up to four hundred yards downrange. Whatever waited for them in the desert camp ahead, al-Kassar thought they were ready.

In fact, he was betting his life on it.

Without the headlights, Sergeant Zureiq had been forced to cut back on their speed. It almost seemed that they were crawling now, giving their targets more than ample opportunity to plan a hot reception for them. But al-Kassar knew they would gain no benefit from racing toward the camp, disabling their vehicles with reckless driving. Save that for their retreat, if they found themselves facing superior force.

He checked his own carbine and pistol, making sure that both had live rounds in their chambers, with their safeties off. He wanted no pathetic fumbling with the weapons if he had to use them, no impediment to killing anyone who threatened him.

He had personally killed a dozen men. Two had been political assassinations, the remainder slain in skirmishes with soldiers. Dozens more had died at his direction, either following his orders or resisting them. None of the deaths weighed on his conscience. They had been sacrifices for a holy cause.

Blood was required to purge his home of tyranny. It was a time for executioners.

"Looks like a camp," Azmeh said, pointing to a glow in the distance.

Bolan scanned the desert with his night-vision goggles, then checked the GPS. "From what I see, the distance fits our beacon signal."

"So, the prisoners."

"If so, they're not alone."

"How many soldiers do you think there are?"

"No telling from this distance," Bolan said. "If they *are* soldiers."

"Rebels should not seek to harm the delegates," said Azmeh.

"If security's in place, they wouldn't know the UN's mission, and they might not care, regardless. All the groups you've got lined up against the regime, some of them fighting one another, I can see one trying to upset the apple cart."

Azmeh sighed. "Yes. If we could all cooperate, the struggle might be over now."

"I doubt there's ever been a revolution without friction on the up-and-coming side. It's human nature. Everybody wants to lead."

"I don't," Azmeh replied. "I want revenge for my family, but I will never know the men responsible. Beyond that, I want peace."

"You still might get it," Bolan told him. "Don't give up."

"I can't. Beyond the struggle, I have nothing left. Sometimes I wonder if my country can recover after so much blood and suffering."

Bolan nodded grimly. He'd seen his share of suffering and knew how hard it could be for people—let alone, nations—to come back from it. That was why he stayed in this game. There would always be criminals and despots who sought to harm others; he did what he could to cut down those players, to give regular people a fighting chance at freedom and justice.

They were drawing closer to the lights now, and Bolan shifted his focus to the immediate task.

"When we're half a mile from contact, we'll proceed on foot," he told his guide. "See what the layout looks like, then decide the best way to move in."

"And if we find the prisoners?"

"Play that bit by ear. Extraction and evasion, if it's possible."

"On foot?"

"I know it's not ideal, but we can't drive up to the camp and ask to have a look around."

"On foot," Azmeh repeated. "With six prisoners."

"If all of them are still alive. That's right."

"You make it sound like child's play."

"Hardly. But it's why I'm here."

"If something happens—"

Bolan cut him off. "You want to go all fatalistic on me, you can wait and guard the car."

"You're right. I'm sorry."

"Don't be sorry," Bolan said. "Be strong. And when the trouble starts, be mean."

11

Captain Fakhri stood and watched the vehicles approaching, one hand on his holstered pistol, wishing that he had taken time to retrieve an AKM from his staff car. General Mourad stood beside him, with Major Farzat to his right, while Sergeant Malki took the place to Fakhri's left.

Across the desert flats, the headlights had not slowed on their approach to Fakhri's camp. Three vehicles, he counted now, led by a small one not unlike his own UAZ-469. Behind it, from its light display, he made out an armored personnel carrier, trailed by a truck. From a distance, they looked like a standard army patrol.

Trust nothing, he thought, and unsnapped his holster. Rebels, and even bandits, had seized military rolling stock since the beginning of the civil war or purchased captured vehicles on the black market. Standard military uniforms were also worn at times by Fakhri's enemies, either in an attempt to deceive authorities or simply because they were the best clothes they could get. If these were rebels, they might well be armed as Fakhri's men were armed—or better, for that matter, thanks to aid from the United States.

"Sergeant," he said, "I want all men on high alert."

"Yes, sir!" Malki replied, and scurried off to emphasize the order.

"If these are regulars, send them away," Mourad said in a low and even tone. "We need no more support, and no more witnesses."

"Yes, sir, " Fakhri replied.

"If they are not…" The general let his thought trail off.

"We're ready, sir," Fakhri assured him, hoping it was true.

The four approaching vehicles had closed to something like a quarter mile, advancing at a steady speed, no sudden charge to raise alarms within the camp. Still, it was odd, the captain thought, that no one in the convoy had attempted radio contact to find out if the camp was friendly or hostile. They weren't expected here and should not be aware of Fakhri's presence in the area, much less his mission. If they were a regular, routine patrol that had happened on the site by chance, the general could pull rank, send them packing in an instant.

But if they were not…

Fakhri glanced at his two APCs, pleased to find their machine guns aimed at the approaching convoy. Ranged along the camp's southern perimeter, some two-thirds of his men stood ready with Kalashnikovs to meet any invaders from the darkness. The remainder—Sergeant Malki would have seen to it by instinct—were on guard around the prisoners and on the other edges of the camp, in case this light display was a distraction from a sly infantry raid.

We're ready, he decided. Or, at least, as ready as they'd ever be.

"You speak first," the general instructed him. "If I must intervene, I shall do so."

"Yes, sir."

It came as no surprise that Mourad did not wish to take the lead, to be identified by anyone who was not present in the camp already. If their bloody business went awry tonight, the general could try to wash his hands of it, deny involvement in the whole affair and lay any blame on Captain Fakhri. But if Mourad thought that Fakhri would submit without a fight...

The vehicles were only a hundred yards away now, the headlights bright in Fakhri's eyes. He slipped on his sunglasses, stepping ahead of Mourad and raising his left hand, the right still resting on his gun.

"That's far enough!"

THE DESERT NIGHT was cool, verging on cold, but that did not prevent the traitor from sweating through his clothes. He was nervous. His hands were tingling, not quite shaking, as he watched the new arrivals drawing closer to their camp. General Mourad and Captain Fakhri had gone out to greet them.

Were these the very friends the traitor had been waiting for since he was shot out of the sky? He reckoned it was possible but could not say. He'd never met the men assigned to meet the UN flight when it went down, and if his luck held, he would not see them again after tonight. They had a job to do, as he did, but he hoped somebody had at least described him to them, so they would not cut him down by accident.

On the other hand, if they were regulars arriving unexpectedly, they offered a unique distraction, one that he could use to make his move against the enemy. If he struck now, while Fakhri and Mourad were otherwise engaged, most of their troops watching the convoy from the desert, he would boost his chances of success. The first shot from his Liberator pepperbox would spark instant confusion, and beyond that—

What?

His death, perhaps, but not before he pinned the general with rifle sights and sent his rotten soul to hell, where it would burn for all eternity.

And if he killed Fakhri as well, so much the better. Two for one, and any more were frosting on the cake.

A voice cut through his thoughts. "Rafic, can you make out what they are saying?"

Rafic Al Din frowned, shook his head. "No, sir. I might try to get closer."

"What?" Qabbani blinked at him. "No, don't do anything to place yourself at risk!"

"We're all at risk," the traitor told him, "every day. Besides, it's time."

Another blink. "I don't know what… Are you all right, Rafic?"

"I've never felt better," Al Din said. And it was true. He felt as if a massive weight had lifted from his shoulders.

"You are not making sense," Qabbani said. "If you feel ill—"

Al Din laughed at him, the sharp sound of it startling in the desert darkness. The nearby guards were turning toward him now, the traitor knew, but he was no longer concerned with them.

"I'm making *perfect* sense," he told Qabbani. "Listen, I believe you are an honest man, a patriot, a *good* man. But your path to victory is hopeless. Surely you must see that now."

"We've had a setback, but—"

"A setback! You're still blind, in spite of everything. Your mission, this weak effort to negotiate, was never going to succeed. Allah does not permit concessions to his enemies. You must be sacrificed and serve our people as a martyr, rather than a weakling in the flesh."

"Rafic—"

"Enough," Al Din said, drawing his 3D-printed pistol. He cocked the clunky-looking gun and shot Qabbani in the face.

THE FIRST SHOT rang out as Bolan stood beside the Niva, suiting up. It was a crisp, sharp sound—a pistol, smaller than 9 mm, though he couldn't peg it any more precisely from a distance. Perhaps two seconds passed, and then more weapons started firing, the distinctive stutter of AKs punctuated by the deeper thuds of several heavy machine guns.

"Sounds like they started the festivities without us," he told Azmeh. "We'd better go and see. You ready?"

"Yes."

They set off from the vehicle, jogging as fast as they could, given the rocky terrain. Speed was important, but not as important as reaching the camp alive and fit for battle.

Bolan saw the muzzle-flashes now, what seemed to be a serious engagement at the site where he had hoped to find the homing beacon and the wayward diplomats. The good news: if two sides were locked in battle, he could try taking advantage of the chaos to retrieve his quarry.

Bad news: by the time he reached the desert camp, the men he'd come to find and rescue could be dead.

Bolan picked up his pace, eyes shifting constantly from the dark ground before him to the battlefield ahead, now less than half a mile away. Once they arrived, they'd stay in cover long enough to gauge the situation, try to find out who was fighting whom, and then they would be in the thick of it—unless he saw immediately that the diplomats were dead.

That seemed unlikely, but he couldn't rule it out. If he did confirm the party had been taken out for good, Bolan would have to choose between punishing those responsible himself, or leaving them to the tender mercies of the enemies they'd already engaged.

But if the team or any members of it still survived, he had no choice.

The mission was to get them out at any cost.

That was a situation he had faced before, too many times. He knew the ropes and what it took to face an overwhelming force, outnumbered and outgunned, in the defense of innocents.

Same old, same old in Bolan's world.

Another day, another chance to die.

NASSER AL-KASSAR HAD been surprised to see how many soldiers he faced at the desert camp. He hesitated as the officers came forward, sitting in his stolen staff car, walkie-talkie raised to give the order for his men to open fire and wondering if he should try to bluff it out instead.

Then, suddenly, a shot was fired somewhere inside the camp.

Al-Kassar flinched, thinking it might be aimed at him, perhaps at his men, then he saw the officers who'd come out to confront him ducking, turning, looking for the shooter. Off to al-Kassar's right, near one of the trucks, he saw some kind of scuffle, and then another muzzle-flash—a pistol, he guessed by its sound.

Al-Kassar seized the opportunity. "Go! Go!" he shouted into his radio, then rolled out of the vehicle, clutching his AKS carbine. Behind and above him, his APC turret gunner was already following orders, raking the camp with fire. He saw one of the regular officers fall, his legs cut from under him, blood everywhere.

His other men were leaping from their vehicles now, finding what cover was available, firing into the camp. The regulars, outnumbering al-Kassar's fighters roughly two to one, were shooting back, but some of them appeared to be distracted by another skirmish inside the camp, where the first shot had gone off.

In a sudden flash of clarity, he yelled to his men, "The prisoners! Don't shoot the prisoners!" If anyone heard him, it was not apparent from their actions. The machine gun on his APC kept sweeping death across the army's ranks. His riflemen continued firing at their enemies.

Under the circumstances, what else could they do?

Al-Kassar himself had wriggled underneath his staff car, cringing as successive bursts of rifle fire kicked sand into his face. The NSV machine guns on the army's two APCs were scoring hits on al-Kassar's vehicles. One slug tore through the radiator of al-Kassar's staff car, releasing a cascade of heated water before shattering the engine block and spilling a mix of oil and gasoline.

There went al-Kassar's ride back to headquarters, if he was still alive to make that journey when the smoke cleared.

And his mission? It was literally being shot to hell.

He had one hope left: to get inside the camp, evading troops who wished to kill him, and find the UN prisoners. He'd still have to extricate them somehow to use them for his own ends, as originally planned.

Or might there be another way?

His plan to stage and carry out an execution to dupe the global media was obviously trashed beyond repair. He could revise that plan, however, by filming the *aftermath* of a supposed execution with a narration claiming that he had come upon government troops too late to save the diplomats and punished those responsible accordingly. He'd have to arrange the bodies properly, strip unit patches from the camouflage fatigues that his men wore, and guard against an errant camera angle.

But it could work.

Feeling a sudden rush of optimism, al-Kassar grinned fiercely, squeezing off a burst of fire into the camp.

It took a moment for Firas Mourad to realize that he was still alive. The blood soaking into his uniform belonged to poor Raed Farzat, his aide, who lay beside him, gasping out his final breaths. Farzat's legs had been shattered—nearly severed outright—by the initial burst of machine gun fire from the incoming vehicles.

But who had fired that first, single shot?

Mourad wasn't particularly interested in the answer at that moment, with bullets from both sides heating the air overhead. Major Farzat's wailing grated on the general's ears like nails on a chalkboard. Mourad considered reaching out to strangle him, but feared that someone might observe him and remember, even in the camp's chaotic state.

His next best option—and by far the safest choice, all things considered—was to crawl away. But where? Dumb luck had placed him on the firing line between two hostile forces. Both sides were dressed in army uniforms, fighting from army vehicles, and Mourad could be mistaken for an infiltrator. If he were killed, who could determine where the shot had come from? Was anyone likely to care?

He started crawling, slowly, trying not to draw attention, careful not to raise his head or buttocks as he wormed across the killing field, clawing with fingers that had lost their manicure, pushing with boots now scuffed and scarred. If he could reach one of the APCs and hide beneath it, he should be secure.

Unless the raiders came equipped with rocket launchers or grenades.

Mourad decided he would worry over that once he found cover and felt reasonably safe. If necessary, should it seem his men were losing to the rebels, he could set off into the desert and dig a hole to hide in while they finished mopping up. It might look bad— Mourad, the sole survivor of a massacre—but he could always slant the story in his favor, maybe claim that he'd been knocked unconscious, overlooked by the rampaging enemy.

The key point was *surviving*. If he managed that, there would be ample time to craft a story while he waited for his rescue party to arrive. Mourad might even find a way to seem heroic when he told the final tale.

He reached the closest APC, its machine gun hammering above him, raining hot brass on to Mourad's scalp and back. He grimaced, dragged himself under the vehicle, then cried out as a sudden, greater pain ripped through the heel of his left foot. A bullet had drilled through his boot, tearing flesh and splintering bone.

Mourad could still hear Major Farzat screaming—or were those his own cries echoing beneath the APC? He bit his tongue, still heard the screams, and started fumbling for the pistol on his Sam Browne belt. If killers came for him, at least he could defend himself.

The Makarov felt reassuring in his hand.

BOLAN AND AZMEH skirted the small convoy, giving it a wide berth. They wouldn't stand a chance charging the skirmish line directly, but with an oblique approach they might manage to penetrate the camp and find the men they had come looking for.

Or find their corpses, anyway.

Each moment that the fight went on decreased the odds of all six diplomats emerging safe and sound. If those who held the prisoners viewed the attack as an attempt to free—or steal—them, they might well be executed on the spot. The flip side of that brutal coin was accidental death, considering all the bullets flying through the camp.

Bolan had no idea which side the two groups of combatants represented, and he didn't care. They were all dressed alike, with standard-issue arms and vehicles.

All of them would, presumably, be glad to kill two interlopers from the darkness. Bolan's aim was to slip
past them with as little fuss as possible and extract his
targets from the melee. Failing that, he'd have to fight
his way out, using any means at his disposal.

Like an APC, for instance, if it came to that.

Azmeh was keeping up so far, not hampered by his
wound. Bolan admired his spirit, hoped it didn't get the
warrior killed, but had no time to focus on him now. A
hundred yards and closing on the camp, he saw what
seemed to be the weak spot he was looking for and angled toward four trucks sitting in a tidy row.

When no one spotted them at fifty yards, he was
encouraged.

By the time they'd closed to twenty yards, he figured
they were in. Not home and dry by any means, but that
much closer to a resolution of their quest. The fight still
raged to their left, but he also heard gunfire within the
camp itself, almost an echo of the main event.

And what did that mean?

Internal fighting might work out to his advantage—
anything that thinned the hostile ranks was good—but
it might also keep him from reaching the diplomats.

He reached the tailgate of a hulking army truck and
paused there for a moment, crouching while the battle sputtered on, some thirty yards away. Azmeh was
close enough that Bolan felt him at his back. Bolan led
them to the narrow gap between this truck and the one
parallel to it.

"Ready?" he asked over his shoulder.

"Ready," Azmeh whispered back.

12

In spite of everything, Rafic Al Din had been surprised
by the effect of his first gunshot. It had been quite effective on Muhammad Qabbani, drilling his left cheek
just below the startled eye and snuffing out his life as
if someone had flipped a light switch. That, Al Din had
expected. But the rest...

Before the echo of his shot had reached the camp's
outskirts, Al Din rounded on the nearest guard assigned
to watch his party, caught the young and slack-jawed
soldier turning toward him, and immediately fired
the second barrel of his Liberator pepperbox into the
guard's forehead. His target crumpled, and Al Din was
quick enough to snatch the dying man's Kalashnikov
before it hit the ground—and that was when his plan
imploded.

All along the camp's southern edge, automatic weapons blazed to life, their thunder shattering the desert
night. Al Din saw men falling, had no time to mourn
the ones who might be rebels like himself. He dropped

his clunky 3D-printed pistol, made sure the Kalashnikov was cocked, and bolted for the nearest BTR-152.

The turret gunner seemed to think the first shots had been fired by someone in the late-arriving party, an assumption shared by nearly all the man's comrades on the skirmish line. His NSV machine gun was the loudest weapon in the grim cacophony, its muzzle-flashes blazing out three feet from the barrel like lightning strikes.

Before Al Din could reach the vehicle, a guard who had seen the traitor kill his colleague raised his AKM to fire from fifteen feet, but Al Din had spent the whole night rehearsing his attack and did not hesitate. He stitched the soldier with a short burst, bullets ripping through the young man's heart and lungs, and turned away without watching him fall.

He stole a quick glance toward the nearby battle zone and picked out the target that preoccupied him now. General Firas Mourad was in the midst of it, not yet fighting himself, but caught up in the middle of the storm. Al Din hoped nobody else would finish the general before he had a chance to do it, and the thought helped speed him toward the nearby army APC.

Two men were crouched behind it, popping up to fire short bursts, then ducking back again to safety. Neither of them saw Al Din coming up behind them, focused as they were on keeping out invaders. When he shot each of them in the back, the best and cleanest way to put them down, they both dropped into bloody heaps with no idea of who had finished them.

Al Din seized the moment, scrambling up the APC's tailgate and over its fat spare tire, one top hatch closed, the other open to accommodate the turret gunner. The traitor leaned across the armored roof and fired into the shooter's back and neck.

The dead machine-gunner slid down inside the APC and Al Din followed him, stepping on one of his twitching legs. He grabbed the NSV's grips, still sweaty from the palms of the man he'd killed a heartbeat earlier.

Al Din rose through the hatch and swung the captured weapon to his left, seeking Firas Mourad—and could not find him.

Where had the sick bastard gone?

MACK BOLAN PAUSED between the front ends of the two trucks and scanned the camp for any sign of those he'd come to rescue. What he saw first was a soldier sprawled on the ground about ten feet in front of him, his face blown off, and then another a few feet beyond that who'd taken several bullets to the chest. Neither had died within direct view of the main battle, and even in the semidarkness, Bolan could tell the face shot had been fired at extremely close range.

The pistol he'd heard before the other shooting started?

Fired by whom, and why?

He crept into the open, Azmeh close behind him. Bolan turned to his right and came upon four members of the UN party huddling nearly within arm's reach. The line of trucks had blocked them from view when he'd done his recon of the camp.

Four out of six accounted for…then he saw that it was five. Muhammad Qabbani was down and out, another close-range shot to the face, likely dead before he hit the hardpan. That left one still missing from the mix.

Before approaching them, Bolan ticked off the names

and faces of the team. Segrest and Walton, check. Sani Bakole and Tareq Eleyan, check. That meant Rafic Al Din was missing, and an ugly image of betrayal formed in Bolan's mind. He didn't know the details, but they hardly mattered.

All that counted now was getting out alive.

The prisoners cringed at first sight of Bolan and Azmeh through the drift of battle smoke. He headed off their questions. "We've come to get you out of here. There's no time for discussion. You've already lost two men, and if you want to live, we have to move right now. Agreed?"

Segrest and the Nigerian UN official shared a glance, both frowning, then nodded in unison. Their aides joined in a second later, making it unanimous.

"Okay," Bolan pressed on. "We'll have to leave Mr. Qabbani and—"

Two soldiers captured his attention, jogging toward them with rifles held across their chests. Bolan raised his AKMS and triggered two short bursts that knocked them into the sand, then turned back to the gaping diplomats.

"As I was saying—time to go."

The how of it was something else. He and Azmeh had hiked in unobserved, but six men exiting the camp on foot were bound to draw attention, even in the middle of a firefight. They were likely to be shot or overtaken long before they reached the Niva SUV, or the vehicle itself would be riddled with bullets if someone managed to get airborne in the gunship parked at the north edge of the camp.

Which gave Bolan a new idea.

"One small diversion coming up," he told Azmeh and

the diplomats as he slipped the RPG off of its shoulder sling. "As soon as this pops, we'll be heading for the nearest APC to hitch a ride."

FIRAS MOURAD THOUGHT he must be hallucinating when he heard a loud voice cursing him by name, somewhere atop the BTR-152 that sheltered him. Was he delirious from pain caused by his bullet wound? Was it the voice of Allah, scolding him for his sins now that his death seemed imminent?

No to the latter, anyway. Mourad did not think Allah would employ such language, even while condemning damned souls to the fires of hell.

"Come out, Mourad, you filthy bastard," the voice called. "You pathetic coward! You butcher! Face me like a man."

Mourad had no intention of emerging from his dusty lair. Whoever was raving overhead, his insults punctuated with machine-gun bursts, the very last thing Mourad would do was show himself, inviting lethal fire.

"I knew you were a fucking coward!" the shouter continued. "Scum!"

Mourad's cheeks flamed at the abuse, but he was not an idiot. He would remain in hiding, safe from the machine gun blasting overhead, and force the screaming maniac to climb down from his high perch if he planned to kill him.

Who was he? How had he assumed possession of the BTR-152? In truth, Mourad cared less for the answers to those questions than for one chance to eliminate his shouting enemy. One shot could do it, if the maniac descended, searching for him.

Mourad did not believe in wishing, but it seemed to

work this time. After one last barrage of insults and obscenities, he heard footsteps above him on the APC's steel floorboard. He could track the howler's movements by those footsteps, knew when he had reached the driver's door and opened it, then stepped onto the dry soil. Instead of clanking, now the footsteps crunched as they circled around the armored vehicle.

"I smell you under there, you rat," said the madman, almost crooning now. "You smell like shit and piss, hiding under there."

Mourad followed the sounds until he caught a glimpse of shoes and trouser cuffs. He gripped his Makarov so tightly that his knuckles cracked, and he worried the sound had given him away.

"Come out, you filthy coward. Face me in your dying moment, General."

Mourad followed the moving feet until they passed from sight, then waited until they reappeared. This time, they stopped approximately level with the spot where Mourad lay concealed, beneath the APC's drive shaft.

Suddenly, the hunter dropped to one knee, and bending lower, poked his head and an assault rifle under the vehicle. "I see you, General!" he crowed, grinning in triumph.

Mourad shot him with the Makarov, its rapid-fire reports numbing his ears. He saw the stranger's face transformed into a grisly mask, but not before the dead man's index finger clenched around the trigger of his rifle.

Muzzle-flashes lit up the underside of the APC, and then Mourad's world went black.

THIS HELICOPTER WAS easier to take out than the last one, sitting still, unoccupied, not strafing Bolan with its autocannon. After making sure the four remaining diplomats were well clear of the RPG's back-blast, he aimed and put his rocket through the bird's windshield and into the cockpit, where it detonated with a clap of smoky thunder, guaranteeing that the Mil Mi-8 would never fly again without a total overhaul.

Job done.

Bolan's next target, while the camp still reeled from his destruction of the helicopter, was the nearest BTR-152. Its turret gun had fallen silent, and it seemed to be unoccupied, although he guessed that wouldn't last for long.

"This way!" he told the others, breaking for the Russian APC. The diplomats trailed him obediently, Sabah Azmeh covering the rear.

His luck held when he reached the APC and found its driver's door wide open. Bolan ducked inside, confirming that no soldiers were hiding there and that he could start the vehicle with a push button instead of a key.

Before starting the engine, Bolan mounted two low metal steps to reach the gun turret. He swung the heavy NSV around to face the second APC in camp, fixing its sights on the machine-gunner who hadn't left his post and whose weapon posed the only real threat to their escape once they'd rolled out of camp.

That shooter never knew what hit him. Bolan's sudden storm of 12.7 mm rounds caught the gunner unaware and ripped his upper body into pieces. When he'd dropped from sight, Bolan glanced down and found his five companions all inside the APC, its door securely shut.

"Do you know how to drive this thing?" he asked Azmeh.

"Yes, sir!" Azmeh answered, smiling.

"Okay, get us out of here. Eastbound. The rest of you lie down. Stay on the floor and brace yourselves. We've got a bumpy ride ahead."

Bolan remained at the NSV, keeping watch for any opponents, as Azmeh fired up the engine, shifted into gear and put the APC in motion, cranking through a U-turn. As far as Bolan knew from scanning maps and satellite photos, no settlements lay on the path he'd chosen from here all the way to the Iraqi border, some one hundred fifty miles due east.

The APC rolled over tents and corpses, its ten tons flattening everything in its path. Living soldiers sprang aside, uncertain what to make of the retreating vehicle, and Bolan let them go. They had enough to do already, with the battle going on, and none tried to obstruct his passage through the camp.

Later, if they won the fight, they might pursue him in their cargo trucks—which matched the APC's top speed of forty-six miles per hour and had larger gas tanks—but the trucks weren't armed, except for whatever weapons their passengers carried. Nor were they armored. If it came to that, he'd make short work of them with the NSV well before they closed to rifle range.

"How much gas do we have left?" he shouted down to Azmeh.

"Three-quarters full."

No sweat on that account, at least. Three-quarters of a tank would give them three hundred miles, still twice the distance from their starting point to the Iraqi border—not that Bolan planned to drive that far. He had another plan in mind, uncertain whether it would work or not, but it was damn sure worth a try.

CAPTAIN FAKHRI THOUGHT the world was ending when the helicopter exploded, struck by a rocket from within his camp. Seconds later, when the fuel tanks blew, a plume of fire blazed into the sky, and for a moment, the camp seemed to be bathed in sunlight.

In that stark light, Fakhri saw that he was losing. Even with his enemies outnumbered two-to-one, ditto on heavy weapons, they were beating him, routing his soldiers who were still alive and fit for battle. It was shameful and infuriating, standing there with bullets whispering around him, waiting for his life and his career to be snuffed out.

But there was worse yet still to come.

Fakhri was moving toward the APCs for cover when he saw one of them turn its NSV machine gun on its neighbor, taking out the other turret gunner with a short burst. Bewildered, Fakhri heard the rogue vehicle's engine roar to life and saw it grinding through an awkward U-turn, batting troops aside with its extended ramming bumper, running over those who fell in its path. It roared through the camp, trailing tattered tent canvas behind it, racing from the battle toward the dark desert.

Fakhri turned to where the prisoners should have been and found them gone, two of their guards lying in bloody heaps. He nearly panicked then, visions of court-martial and execution flashing through his mind, until the sheer absurdity of that struck him and actually made him laugh.

He was unlikely to survive the next ten minutes, much less face a military trial, unless he took dramatic action on his own to end the firefight and retrieve his prisoners. In spite of everything, he *could* complete his mission if he had the strength and courage required.

Fakhri ran toward the second APC, yanked its door open and crawled in, slipping on blood and brains to reach the turret with its NSV machine gun. There, he checked the ammo box and swung the weapon toward his enemies south of the camp. Their ranks were thinning, and their lead vehicle was in flames. They only needed one last push to finish them. Captain Bassam Fakhri was determined to provide it.

Grinning like a maniac, he held down the machine gun's trigger, raking deadly fire along the tattered skirmish line. He did not count the moving targets, barely noticed as they lurched, jerked and toppled to the ground with 12.7 mm bullets ripping through their flesh. Watching the slaughter, Fakhri's men regrouped and found their courage once again, raised battle cries and charged their enemies.

In moments, it was over. Fakhri ducked inside the APC to grab the microphone from the dashboard. "Quiet!" he shouted, his voice booming through the camp. "Listen! Our prisoners are fleeing. If we cannot get them back, we all face trial for dereliction of our duty!"

Sobered in an instant, waiting for his order, his surviving soldiers gave Fakhri their rapt attention.

"Join me!" he commanded. "We'll go after them and bring them back. The mission can be saved!"

Sergeant Malki answered first, appearing out of nowhere through the battle smoke. "I'll drive, Captain," he said. "What are we waiting for?"

"Who are you?" Robert Segrest asked when the camp was a mile or more behind them. "Where'd you come from?"

"State can brief you when they're ready," Bolan answered from the driver's seat. "Right now, I need to use the radio."

"Now, see here—"

"Go sit down," Bolan commanded, in a voice that brooked no argument. Segrest seemed to be on the verge of saying more, then reconsidered and returned to his bench seat on the left side of the APC's spacious troop compartment. Sabah Azmeh had the turret, facing backward just in case.

Bolan checked the dashboard-mounted two-way radio's setting before he palmed the microphone. He confirmed the radio's frequency was set for International Telecommunication Union Region 1, including all of Europe, Russia, Africa and the Middle East west of Iran.

A thousand ears might pick up Bolan's broadcast, but he didn't care, as long the right ears were listening in Baghdad.

The CIA was still in place in the city, reporting each attack, each bombing, each new skirmish back to Washington. They were supposed to be on board for Bolan's mission, handling the lift-out if he made it that far, but experience had taught him that the agency was not always reliable.

However, right now, they appeared to be the only game in town.

"Striker calling Backfire," Bolan said into the microphone, repeating it three times before an answer came back.

"Backfire reading. Over."

"Calling in for pickup as agreed," Bolan replied. "Over."

"Roger that, Striker. We'll need coordinates for pickup."

"Wait one," Bolan said, and checked his GPS. He had a spot in mind, picked out on Google Earth for isolation and accessibility. He double-checked coordinates and gave them back to Baghdad.

"Liftoff within fifteen," the voice of Backfire told him. "Pickup estimated within sixty-five."

Minutes, that was. They had to stay alive for one more hour and be waiting at the pickup site he had arranged.

No problem. Unless the Syrians came after them.

As if in answer to his thought, Azmeh bent down from his turret post. "I see headlights."

13

There were enough men left in camp to fill the eighteen seats aboard the BTR-152, with Sergeant Malki driving and Captain Fakhri in the shotgun seat. Their enemies had a head start, but it was not extreme, no more than twenty minutes. Fakhri believed he could overtake the fleeing APC, but first they had to find it, which meant spotting lights in the vast, dark desert that surrounded them.

Searching the night with narrowed eyes, he let his mind drift to the questions that were haunting him: Who had absconded with his prisoners, and why?

There seemed to be three possibilities. First, rebels from the party he'd defeated could have done it, two or three of them dispatched to infiltrate the camp while the majority distracted Fakhri and his soldiers. As to why rebels might flee eastward with the hostages, he could not say. In the short term, simply escaping from the army camp might be their goal—in which case, they weren't likely to continue east for any great distance, and Fakhri might have lost their trail already.

Second—a far-fetched idea, but still conceivable—another army unit might have been dispatched to claim the prisoners without his knowledge, and perhaps without Mourad's. He could not ask the general; Mourad had been found dead with one of the six diplomats who had seemingly run amok during the firefight, killing several soldiers in a fruitless effort to break free. If regular commandos were involved, their eastward flight from camp could simply be an effort to avoid the firefight prior to striking off for whatever part of the country they called home base.

And what would that mean, if the army trusted Fakhri so little that they would give him an assignment, then snatch it away clandestinely?

The answer to that question could be grim indeed.

But still, it was the third option that troubled Fakhri most. If outsiders had taken the prisoners, where had they come from? Who'd sent them? How had they penetrated Fakhri's camp unnoticed, even with a firefight going on? And most importantly, where would they take the hostages?

Fakhri believed he knew the answer to the last question, at least. The plane bearing his former prisoners had flown in from Iraq, whose feeble government was still in thrall to the United States. The White House, Fakhri knew from the reports he'd heard over Damascus Radio, hated Syria's president and wished to see him dead or groveling in muck. The so-called "diplomatic mission" had been geared to that result. Why wouldn't Western agents try to save the spies, once the trip had gone awry?

Now Fakhri had a choice to make. If he believed the third idea, it meant his enemies were fleeing toward Iraq, but he still needed to find them in the desert.

Syria's border with Iraq was nearly four hundred miles long, but no sensible fugitive would run to the extremes of north or south. Realistically, Fakhri thought he had a forty- or fifty-mile front to worry about, and a relatively straight run to the border seemed most likely, on or near the course he had already set.

In theory, if he was correct, all Fakhri had to do was hold that course and watch for lights ahead, then do his best to overtake the stolen APC.

Which, he realized, could be a challenge in itself.

The BTR-152s were matched in terms of armor and defensive weapons. He might have more soldiers, but they did Fakhri no good in a motorized chase. If anything, there was a chance their extra weight might slow his progress just enough to give the enemy a slim advantage when it came to speed. And if he lost them…

I might as well keep going, Fakhri said to himself. Surrender at the border, seek asylum and be done with it.

The foolish thought struck Captain Fakhri like a slap across the face. He stiffened in his seat and refocused on the pitch-black night in front of him, searching for any sign to give him hope.

And had a sudden inspiration.

"Malki, kill the headlights!" he commanded.

"Sir?" The sergeant sounded both confused and worried. "We could crash, or—"

"Do it!"

"Yes, sir."

Malki did as he was told.

BOLAN CHECKED THE mirror and saw a single pair of headlights following his dust trail several miles back. Then, suddenly, they winked out.

"They're gone!" Azmeh called down to him.

"I see that."

Bolan weighed the odds of a coincidental follower and judged that they were nil. But it would be suicide to drive without headlights on this terrain. The fact that they'd been using the high beams at all suggested they didn't have night-vision technology. Bolan saw only two possibilities. The chase vehicle could have crashed into a wadi or a boulder, or the driver was trying to run a stealth maneuver on the enemy.

Too late for that, but with their lights out, the pursuers *could* gain ground without Bolan observing them, at least until they'd closed the gap enough to open fire.

He checked the APC's speedometer and saw that they were maxed out. Remembering the vehicles he'd seen in camp, there had been only one—the UAZ-469—that had a slight edge on the APC for speed, at fifty miles per hour maximum.

The down side for his enemies, if they'd chosen the land rover, was that it carried no machine gun mount. Its armament on contact would be limited to small arms carried by its passengers—unless, that is, one of them had the foresight to include an RPG.

The other APC in camp would have more trouble catching him, but it could carry twenty soldiers, and it had an NSV machine gun in its turret. They'd be matched on firepower in that case, and it could go either way.

Bolan had a choice: run it out and lead them to the pickup site, or stand and deal with it right now.

Turning the options over in his mind, Bolan pressed down on the accelerator, grinding through the endless desert night.

CAPTAIN FAKHRI COULD see the fleeing taillights better with his own headlights turned off. They looked like red rat's eyes. It galled Fakhri to know that they belonged to his own APC, now diverted into the service of his enemies.

Whoever *they* were.

He still had no idea, but he had nearly given up on caring. In an ideal situation, Fakhri would have loved to capture them alive, retrieve the prisoners, and grill their rescuers until he knew the story of their lives, the names and nationalities of their employers, why they had been sent to torment him. But the odds of that occurring were slim to none.

His best bet was simply to annihilate the opposition, along with the four surviving captives they had rescued. Fakhri had not thought to bring the video equipment with him, in his haste to overtake the rescue party, but that hardly mattered now. His scheme had been derailed beyond repair, becoming a debacle, and he would be lucky to survive when he reported back to headquarters. As for promotion, decoration, all those other cherished fantasies—forget it.

He would never rise above his present rank and was unlikely to retain it very long. If he avoided a court-martial and a hangman's noose, Fakhri would offer prayers of thanks to Allah for his blessings.

How he hated them, these strangers he had never met. Without a passing thought for Fakhri, they had crept into his life and fouled it, like a burglar who not only steals but also feels compelled to vandalize a home before he slinks away. His rage was limitless. Given the chance, he could annihilate a thousand men and still not be appeased.

But there were not a thousand men inside the fleeing APC. Four former prisoners and…what? No more than two or three combatants at the most, he guessed. Fakhri, with nineteen men behind him, should have no great difficulty killing them.

And yet…

He could not shake his anxiety, a sense of overlooking something that could easily rebound to damage him. No matter how he tried to focus in the noisy, jolting APC, the kernel of his thought eluded him.

One more spark of fury added to the crackling flame inside his head. If he could just—

Ahead of them, the taillights vanished.

Fakhri blinked and found his eyes were not deceiving him. The red pinpricks were gone.

"What happened?" he asked Sergeant Malki.

"I don't know, sir. Maybe they saw our lights go off?"

"You're asking me?"

"No, sir. A thought."

"What if we lose them now?"

Reluctantly, his driver said, "It's possible."

"Fuck! We're losing them. They are escaping as we speak."

"What would you have me do, sir? Shall we stop and listen?"

"Listen?"

"For their engine, sir."

"Listen," Fakhri repeated through clenched teeth. "What if they've switched their engine off?"

"At least they would not be escaping, sir."

Fakhri's mind reeled, hearing such lunacy. But could he think of something better?

Agonizing seconds passed, their APC still rolling eastward at its best speed, given the terrain. Fakhri was tortured by the possibility of missing their quarry, passing right by them in the darkness without ever noticing.

What else could go wrong?

"Screw this," he said at last. "Turn on the headlights!"

"THEY'RE BACK!" the Arab gunman called down from his turret. "The lights are back!"

"I see them," said the driver, sounding more relaxed than any human should, under the circumstances.

Roger Segrest watched him, wishing he could ask a dozen different questions, but the driver frightened him. Segrest had seen him shoot men, heard more screaming as the armored vehicle ran over them, and when the driver had told them all to lie down and be quiet, Segrest didn't have the nerve to argue with him. This was not some flunky he could pull rank on and push around. The man was homicidal, highly trained—and he was saving Segrest's life.

Or trying to, at least.

Lights on their trail meant a pursuit, which meant more fighting and a possibility that Segrest could be injured, even killed. He cursed the mission that had brought him here, where he could glimpse the end of his life.

If I get through this shit, he promised himself, I'm done.

He'd pack it in, go back to teaching history at some posh university, and start working on his memoirs. This ordeal would be a gripping chapter, and if he came out sounding more heroic than he'd ever been...well, what would be the harm in that?

"Sir, who *are* these people?" Dale Walton whispered.

"Hell if I know," Segrest answered softly. "But at least they're on our side."

"Are they?"

And how was he supposed to answer that? The driver and his buddy had come out of nowhere, suddenly appearing in the army camp as if they'd sprung up from the desert sand itself. They'd taken charge, mowed down the men who had been holding Segrest and his fellow diplomats against their will, and snatched them out of there.

So far, so good, but Segrest still had no idea who they were or who had sent them, where they planned on taking him or why. Was this in fact a rescue, or another kidnapping? What should he think of men who killed so ruthlessly?

They're soldiers, Segrest reassured himself. But whose?

Not Navy SEALS or Green Berets, that much was obvious.

They could be mercenaries working under contract— but again, for whom? Segrest knew that his government used private contractors for dirty jobs around the world, to fill in where the military couldn't go and thus preserve deniability. Something he took for granted, working for the State Department, and which rarely bothered Segrest as he went about his normal rounds in Washington. But this was different; the blood was real.

And why did he feel guilty about still being alive?

"We're going eastward," Sani Bankole informed him. "Iraq, perhaps?"

That worked for Segrest, and it helped explain the cryptic words their driver had exchanged by radio with someone he called "Backfire."

Segrest allowed himself a spark of hope but didn't let it flare out of control. He would feel safe again when they were all behind barbed wire, surrounded by Americans and waiting for a flight back to the States.

Until then, he was just another moving target in the hostile night.

BOLAN HAD TRICKED his enemies, hitting the kill switch for his taillights, running dark just long enough to make them nervous back there in the chase car. And they'd bitten.

But after confirming their pursuers hadn't given up the chase, Bolan still had the same life-or-death dilemma: flee or fight?

Their pickup out of Baghdad would be in the air by now, or very shortly, but that left an hour yet to go before contact. Bolan didn't know what they'd be flying, but he couldn't count on armored gunships swooping to the rescue, and it felt wrong leading enemies to crash the party when they might kill good men he'd never met.

The other side of that coin: he could stop, turn back and face whoever was following them. He didn't doubt that he could pull it off with Azmeh's help, but if their vehicle was damaged and could not proceed, it meant a long walk to Iraq with no pickup and hostiles snapping at their heels along the way.

Bad choices, with no third alternative, but Bolan couldn't put it off much longer. The headlights in his wing mirror seemed to be a little closer than the last time he had seen them. They weren't gaining rapidly, but they were hanging in there, ready to stick it out for the long haul.

Bolan did the calculations swiftly. If he turned around right now, the chase vehicle would be within range of his NSV machine gun. Barely, but that was better than nothing. As far as *aiming* at that range with open sights, his target close to a mile and a half downrange in darkness—that would be a crapshoot. He might stop the camp's staff car, one of the trucks, but if the hunters were inside the second BTR-152, it was a different story.

The enemy needed to be closer for decisive hits, and that would mean exposing his ride and its passengers to equal danger.

If they were in the APC.

The bottom line: he didn't know what they were driving, and he couldn't know until they'd closed to killing range. He didn't want to take that risk, but if he led a hostile armored vehicle to his pickup site and the collection team showed up in something like your basic Huey chopper, with no armor anywhere except beneath the pilots' seats, he'd be responsible for the ensuing carnage.

Choices.

And he'd have to make one soon.

14

"The border's coming up in…five…four…three…"

Jeff Baxter finished off the countdown as they crossed the line and entered Syria, skimming the desert floor at thirty feet to frustrate any radar outposts in the neighborhood.

"We're in it now," Ward Simmons said from the co-pilot's seat.

Behind them, Craig Rowe whooped into his mic.

"This isn't a hunting party," Baxter answered back. "Just keep your eyes peeled."

"Roger that," Rowe answered, grinning.

They were riding in an Aérospatiale SA 330 Puma out of Baghdad. The chopper had a range of some three hundred sixty miles, no sweat on that score, and a maximum speed of 159 miles per hour. Their service ceiling was close to sixteen thousand feet, but they wouldn't be coming anywhere near that altitude this time around, with the hush-hush proviso from Backfire.

Stealth was essential for the people they were going

to collect and for the whirlybird itself. The Puma had no armor, and it was officially unarmed, though Rowe was ready with an FN Minimi light machine gun chambered in 5.56×45 mm NATO. Besides the Minimi, all three crewmen were packing Glock 22s, the .40 S&W models, with a pair of Heckler & Koch MP5 SMGs in reserve.

Unarmed my ass, thought Baxter. As if anyone would enter Syria that way.

Baxter didn't know who they were picking up or why they needed a lift back to Baghdad, and he couldn't care less. As a contract employee, he flew where he was told, made pickups and drop-offs without asking questions, and smiled all the way to the bank. His life had travel and adventure, with enough time off to spend some of the money he was paid for taking risks.

Like now.

Once they were in Syrian airspace, anything could happen. If MiGs caught a whiff of them, it wouldn't even be a fight, with the jet fighters' vastly superior weapons and speed. Baxter could try to dodge incoming fire and might succeed in the short run, but anyone who backed the Puma against jets must be an idiot with a death wish.

It would be half an hour, give or take, before they reached the pickup zone. Their orders were to grab whoever made it to the site but not to wait around for any stragglers. Getting caught in Syria meant more than losing personnel, as everyone aboard the chopper knew only too well. It meant *exposure*, something that the Company despised and would not tolerate. If they were nabbed across the line and managed to survive, there would be no rescue attempts and no exchanges. Langley would deny all knowledge of them, naturally, and the Puma's crew had no ID on board. Their chopper, if dismantled and examined, could be traced back to its registered owners in Zurich but not one step beyond.

They were, for all intents and purposes, inside the Twilight Zone.

And whether they would make it back was anybody's guess.

THE BTR-152S HAD no reflectors on their tailgates, but when Sergeant Malki switched the headlights on once more, Fakhri made out an image, like a ghostly echo of his own vehicle, ahead of them. It trailed a rooster tail of dust and seemed intent on speed, rather than evasion.

"More speed!" Fakhri barked.

"Captain—"

"More speed!"

Malki did what he could, pressing the APC's accelerator pedal to the floor, hunching forward as if his thoughts alone could squeeze a few more miles per hour from its straining 110-horsepower engine. It was futile, as Fakhri understood too well, but still he ground his teeth and muttered curses as they failed to close the gap between themselves and their quarry.

"Corporal!" he shouted to the turret gunner. "Fire for effect!"

Malki glanced over at him, no doubt thinking that the range was too extreme, but he said nothing. Overhead, the NSV machine gun belched a short exploratory burst, its tracers arcing off beyond the reach of Fakhri's headlights, then began to hammer steadily, its hot brass raining down into the APC.

They might be wasting ammunition, but they were also challenging the fugitives, alerting them to the futility of fleeing. Where did they expect to go? Did they believe a Syrian vehicle under fire would be allowed to cross the border and seek refuge in Iraq, if they could even reach that goal? They had another eighty miles or more to go—nearly two hours at their present speed—and Fakhri meant to hound them every yard along the way, unless they turned to face him.

Then, what?

He had them outnumbered and outgunned. Four of those inside the fleeing APC were mere civilians. Even if they'd picked up weapons from his camp, they would be inexperienced at combat. Any military veterans among them would be years—perhaps decades—beyond training and active service, weakened over time by desk jobs and the soft lives of professional negotiators.

But the other two or three...

They worried Fakhri. Not only because they'd crept into his camp unseen and snatched his captives out from underneath his nose, but for the way they'd taken down so many of his men, hijacked the APC, and managed their escape while under fire. That told him they were brave, skilled and totally professional.

His soldiers, on the other hand, were mostly young conscripts serving their mandatory eighteen months in uniform, fed up with war against their fellow countrymen. Some tens of thousands of soldiers had deserted since the civil war began, including dozens of generals. Fakhri kept close watch on his men each time they left their barracks, even those who'd reenlisted for a five-year stint, uncertain whether he could trust them.

And he swore, if any of them tried to run tonight, he would annihilate the cowards with his own two hands.

SABAH AZMEH DROPPED down from the open turret as a ragged line of tracers rattled overhead. A couple of the bullets struck the APC's tailgate, but the pursuers were too far away to inflict any serious damage.

So far.

Bolan had made his choice. He would not lead the enemy to intercept his rescue flight. That meant a showdown in the desert. There were serious risks and they'd lose precious time, but he saw no alternative. Evasion only burned more fuel and put them farther from the pickup site.

Azmeh slid into the shotgun seat, lowered his voice and asked, "What do we do?"

"Get rid of them," Bolan replied, as two or three more rounds connected with the APC, dimpling its armor.

"And the helicopter?"

Bolan shot a quick glance at the simple dashboard clock. "We should just about have time to meet it, if we wrap this up in ten or fifteen minutes."

That could be a lifetime under fire, and he wasn't sure if he could trust the four civilians not to bolt in panic when the APC started taking full-on hits.

"Can you drive this thing?" he asked Azmeh.

His guide nodded. "Let's switch."

It was an awkward move, hard not to stall the APC's engine, but they got through it, losing speed in the process.

Bolan turned to his passengers. "Who wants to survive and see their families again? Come on. I want a show of hands."

Four hands went up. Four worried faces stared at him.

"We have to stand and fight," he said. "That's it, the

bottom line. I want you all down on the floor. Stay flat, no matter what happens, unless we catch on fire. Then pile out through the back. Understand?"

Four dumb nods. Segrest seemed on the verge of saying something, but he didn't get the chance.

"Right, then," said Bolan, turning back to Azmeh. "I'll be in thc turrct. Bring us back around, as sharp as you can turn it without rolling. Aim the headlights back their way, then drop under the dash. The engine block should cover you."

"But I—"

"Whatever happens, keep an eye on them," Bolan instructed, thumb cocked toward the rear deck, where the diplomats were busy lying down and covering their heads with folded arms. "Don't let them out unless you think the vehicle's about to blow. If that happens, you're on your own."

"And you?"

"Won't matter, then. We're all in," Bolan told him. "Betting everything we've got."

Azmeh nodded. "Whenever you're ready."

"Give me a second to get up there," Bolan said, "then do it."

Leaping for the open turret, Bolan took the NSV machine gun's grips and hung on as the BTR-152 slowed slightly, then began its jolting U-turn back to face their enemies.

ROGER SEGREST WAS furious and terrified, the two emotions grappling for control of his mind and body. Lying facedown on filthy steel, where countless combat boots had left their smears of mud, sand and God knew what else, Segrest thought he was about to die. He felt a pressing need to void his bladder, clamped his thighs together in response and crossed both arms above his head for whatever protection they might offer.

Not much, he supposed, if armor-piercing bullets found their way inside the vehicle. He might not be a soldier, but he'd toured battlegrounds after the fact, seen armored cars and trucks burned out and shot to hell, still reeking of their former occupants. He'd seen what bullets did to flesh and bone.

The last thing Segrest wanted was to die here, in this desert wasteland, six thousand miles from home. But there was nothing he could do about it now. He had to trust the soldiers who had rescued him, do as the man in charge commanded, maybe use the time he had left to sort through his life and find some fleeting trace of inner peace.

That almost made him laugh out loud, but they were swerving now, making him drop one hand to clutch a strut beneath the bench seats to keep from sliding across the floor. The driver took them through a rough one-eighty, facing back the way they'd come, while his companion manned the turret, nothing but his backside and his long legs visible inside the APC.

Risking his life for Segrest and the others, yes. It was what soldiers did to earn their meager paychecks. Segrest definitely yearned to see the last of Syria, but not if that meant being shot to ribbons and going home in a plastic bag.

The gunner had instructed them to stay flat, no matter what happened, unless the APC caught fire. That prospect frightened Segrest more than being shot. It was a nightmare come to life.

Dale Walton lay near Segrest, their heads almost

touching. The aide muttered something underneath his breath. A prayer? Segrest had no idea if Walton was religious, didn't delve into the private lives of his subordinates unless there was a problem that affected job performance, but it still surprised him.

What was it religious people liked to say? No atheists in foxholes. Segrest seriously doubted that, and personally, he thought it was hypocritical to ask some deity for help at times of crisis when you had ignored him or her for most of your life. It smacked of childish desperation, rather than devotion.

No, Segrest decided, he was not going to pray. Instead, he'd focus on his wife and children, hoping that they loved him and would think of him with fondness if—

The big machine gun overhead exploded into action, and his mind shut down.

"THEY'VE TURNED THEIR lights back on," Sergeant Malki said.

"I'm not blind!" Fakhri snapped. His mind was racing, filled with clashing questions. Had the fleeing driver feared crashing his stolen vehicle? It was a real threat in the eastern desert, where rain was rare but fell in torrents when it came, cutting channels through dry, hard-packed soil.

Was the driver taunting Fakhri? And if so, to what purpose? He only made his vehicle a better target with the lights on.

"Hold steady! *Aim*, you idiot!" Fakhri shouted up at the gunner.

His corporal, caught up in the excitement, called

back, "*You* hold steady! How can I hit anything, the way this thing is jerking under me?"

The firing stopped then, both men startled by the gunner's insubordination. After three long seconds, the corporal ducked down to come face-to-face with his captain. "I'm sorry! Please accept—"

"Go back to shooting," Fakhri raged at him, already planning how he would reward the corporal for his lapse in military etiquette.

"Yes, sir!"

The loud machine-gun fire resumed a moment later, and it seemed the tracer rounds *were* flying straighter, after all. Fakhri saw two more strike the APC in front of them, though neither slowed it down. He wished they would ignite the gasoline tank and incinerate the vehicle, together with its passengers. Inspiration struck him, and he turned back toward the turret. "Try for the fuel can on the tailgate. You see it?"

"Yes, sir!" came the crisp reply.

He knew the corporal was lying. Details were a blur, at best, with so much dust rising behind the APC they were pursuing, but spare gas cans always rode the same position on the tailgate of a BTR-152, on a little metal shelf beside the spare tire. A shooter didn't literally have to *see* the can to know where it was located. If he could see the spare—or see the tailgate, for that matter—he could score a hit and light a tail of flame. If only—

Up ahead, the stolen armored car veered slightly. It lost speed, though the brake lights were not flaring. Fakhri wondered if a bullet might have found the driver somehow, against all odds, but then the APC straightened its course, picked up speed, and—

"Look! They're turning!" Fakhri told his driver.

"Neither one of us is blind," Malki replied, tight-lipped.

Another name appended to the insubordination list, but Fakhri let it pass for now, watching the BTR-152 loop through a wide U-turn, its driver matching speed with a concern for tipping over, raising even larger clouds of dust around it. High beams cut a sweeping path through all that dust and sand, veering around to face Fakhri, lancing his eyes.

They've stopped to fight, he thought, and almost smiled before a sudden pang of fear deflated his excitement.

Why would they stop, knowing Fakhri must have fighting men on board, that they would be outnumbered two or three to one? Why not keep running, maybe find a better place with cover somewhere out here?

Captain Fakhri's thoughts evaporated as the other APC's machine gun came to life, its muzzle-flashes blinking at him, spewing rounds directly toward his face.

EYES NARROWED AGAINST rising dust and grit, Bolan locked his knees and hung on while Azmeh completed the wide turn, bringing them back into line with the chase car.

When they straightened out, Bolan was ready, crouching slightly, aiming through the graduated sight atop his NSV. He stroked the trigger lightly, sending half a dozen tracer rounds downrange, and then corrected slightly before letting rip with everything he had, a thunderstorm of 12.7 mm rounds flying to greet the enemy.

The NSV's strong point was power. It could reach

out to two thousand yards, turning men into stew meat before they knew what hit them. Its weakness was the cyclic rate of fire. The standard ammo box, with its disintegrating belt, held only fifty rounds. Full-auto fire exhausted that supply in roughly four seconds, mandating frequent replacement.

Bolan had used part of the NSV's first belt at the camp, while taking out the turret gunner on the second APC, and he was burning through the rest of it right now. Below him sat six more ammo boxes, a total of three hundred rounds remaining.

Would it be enough?

Maybe.

He sighted on the charging APC's wide grill, hood and windshield. Holding steady as his own vehicle stopped, he rattled off the remnants of the ammo box and hoped his enemies were catching hell inside their iron coffin.

A few more seconds, and they would be sending hell right back at him.

Bolan unhooked the empty ammo box and tossed it overboard, stooping to hoist another as his adversary opened fire. The BTR-152's armor, though thickest at the nose, was still vulnerable to the force of the 12.7 mm slugs. He heard them landing, almost randomly at first, and waited for the screams below him that would mark a hit.

None came before he straightened up, attached the second ammo box, and fed its too-short belt into the NSV's receiver. Once the hatch on top was closed, he cocked it, sighted on the other APC's gun turret, and released another swarm of tracers across no-man's land.

Taking the gunner out—or better yet, his gun—was

Bolan's first priority. He didn't think the other APC would ram them head-on, risking damage to itself, since both of them sported the same extended, reinforced bumpers. In theory, they could butt heads all night long, scrambling the brains of their passengers but otherwise achieving squat.

The gunner first, and then the driver. If he got that far, Bolan could win this crazy game of chicken.

15

Sabah Azmeh hit the APC's brake pedal, coming out of their broad turn, and straightened out the steering wheel. He knew he had it right when headlights glared into his eyes and fiery tracers arced away to either side. Reaching up for the control handle, he dropped both windshield shutters with a loud metallic clang.

It was the best protection he could manage in the circumstances, knowing that any of the bullets flying toward him now could still penetrate the armored shutters and the so-called bulletproof glass behind them if the rounds scored a direct hit. He could be killed at any second, but he still peered through the narrow viewing slit to watch the light show.

Azmeh felt trapped, holding the worst seat in the APC right now, and there was nothing he could do about it. Cooper might require his aid, and if that call came, he needed to be ready for it, clear on where his adversaries were positioned and the distance between their vehicles.

Not that it would matter, if they killed him first.

He hated feeling like a stationary target in a shooting gallery.

When the first round pierced his windscreen shutters, missing Azmeh's face by inches, he dove sideways, sprawling across his own seat and the one he'd vacated to take the steering wheel when Cooper went topside. Azmeh thought of what the tall American had said, about the engine block preventing slugs from reaching him, and hoped that it was true.

Behind him, from the steel deck, one of the Americans raised his voice to ask, "What's happening?"

Azmeh, who thought it should be bloody obvious, ignored him, concentrating on the left foot he had braced against the APC's brake pedal, hoping that the tremors in his leg did not allow that foot to slip and stall the engine.

Overhead, there was another break in firing, and he heard Matt Cooper scrabbling for another box of ammunition. That left four, by Azmeh's count, and their enemy was firing at an equal rate. If anyone was still alive when they ran out of bullets, what were they to do?

Jump out, perhaps, and fight with carbines, pistols, even hand-to-hand. It would be brutal, primitive, but even in his nearly paralyzing fear, Azmeh supposed it might be best. Better, at least, than cringing in a ventilated tin can, waiting for his life to end.

Again, the peevish voice called out to Azmeh: "What's he doing? Can't we just get out of here?"

Half turning where he lay, Azmeh snapped back, "He's risking his life to save yours. Shut up and leave him to it, will you?"

The release of pent-up anger freed him. Suddenly and irresistibly, Sabah Azmeh began to laugh.

CAPTAIN BASSAM FAKHRI was terrified. He had been anxious many times during his army tenure, frightened badly on occasion during armed engagements, but this was the first time in his adult life that he had felt stark, raving terror. Crouched as best he could beneath his seat, listening to the hammer strokes of 12.7 mm bullets pounding on the BTR-152 and drilling through its armor, Fakhri thought he was about to die.

And he was not prepared to enter Paradise after his failure on the most important mission of his whole career.

Beside him, Sergeant Malki was already gone. A bullet through the APC's windscreen had slammed through Malki's forehead, taking out a hand-sized portion of his skull in back.

He had already tried the two-way radio, but only static answered him. His sat-phone, curse it, was still sitting in his staff car, foolishly forgotten in his haste to follow the escaping prisoners. Fakhri had no way to report his situation or to ask for help. He could not even tell headquarters where he was about to die.

At least, he thought, General Mourad had gone down first. Fakhri had never liked him, not that anybody gave a fig for his opinion. It pleased him to imagine how the brigadier had felt, seeing his great plan fall to pieces, knowing that his life was at an end. That vision satisfied the captain only long enough to realize that he was wasting time.

Fakhri decided he had to run, if that was still an option. He could try, at least, leave the prisoners to go their own way and fabricate a story that his soldiers would support once they all realized that he had saved their lives.

Or would they blame him for deserting in the face of hostile fire, when they were questioned?

Fakhri struggled to turn, his cramped position on the floorboard shooting darts of pain along his spine, just as another burst of bullets struck the APC. He saw one of his soldiers die, his left arm nearly severed at the shoulder, gushing blood on to the other men nearby.

"Who wants to stay and fight?" Fakhri called out to the remaining troops.

Grim eyes in bloodstained faces studied him with fear and curiosity. No one replied. No hands were raised.

"Or should we just get out of here?" he asked them.

"Go!" one shouted back.

"Get out!" another croaked.

It instantly became a chorus, no dissenters, two or three men pounding fists against the metal floor for emphasis.

"Right," said Fakhri. "We'll be going, then."

If he could drive the APC.

First thing, he had to get rid of Malki's corpse. Fakhri rose from the floorboard, leaned across his driver's mutilated form, and opened up his door. Next, he rolled back and used his feet to push the sergeant's dead weight out and down, into the sand. As soon as Malki was clear, Fakhri replaced him in the driver's seat, cringing as blood and other fluids soaked his trousers.

The motor was still running—raggedly, but holding on. He began to back away, still under fire, then switched gears and cranked the steering wheel hard left, into a turn that kept his side from being exposed. It would be madness for the enemy to follow him at this point, when escape was in their grasp.

Fakhri felt a shout of triumph rising in his throat but

swallowed it. They weren't safe yet, by any means, and would not be until their vehicle was well beyond the other machine gun's killing range.

BOLAN SAW SOMETHING tumble from the other APC, a limp form falling out the driver's door. A second later, as the army gunner stooped to reach another ammo box, the vehicle lurched forward, then seemed to think better of it, motor clanking as it switched into reverse and started backing up.

Retreating or maneuvering?

Bolan had no time to consider options as the turret gunner surfaced once again, reloading from a crouch that only left his two hands and his face exposed.

It was enough.

Bolan squeezed off a burst that emptied his own ammo box, saw blood erupting from the other turret like a fountain as he took the shooter's head off. What was left of him dropped back inside the BTR-152, his death grip slackening, leaving the NSV machine gun pointing skyward.

Bolan took the opportunity to reload, snapped the lid down on the NSV's receiver, cocked it and was ready when the APC in front of him began to make a U-turn, its six tires digging in for traction on the dry hardpan. He strafed those tires and quickly shredded all three on his side. The vehicle slumped like a drunken man, rims grinding into dirt and sand, while Bolan raised his weapon's sights to rake the right side of the APC.

Thin armor on the sides was a design flaw, and he took advantage of it, tracing two long lines of 12.7 mm holes between the front side door and the tailgate. He aimed low, guessing that the smart ones would be flat-tened on the floorboards, the careless ones already dead.

No screams reached Bolan's ears over the hammer-ing of his machine gun, but he pictured hellish scenes inside the APC, supported by his prior experience. When armor failed, fighting machines were nothing more than death traps for the troops inside, penned up like cattle in a slaughterhouse.

He swung back toward the APC's engine compart-ment and used up the rest of his belt there, taking the ZIS six-cylinder mill out of action for good. The for-mer chase car lurched and died, a plume of white smoke curling from beneath its ventilated hood.

Now was the moment to consider his next step. He could drive off and leave the enemy to their fate, what-ever that might be, or he could verify that there were no survivors waiting for a chance to snipe at his vehicle when it retreated.

The decision was made for him, when the BTR's rear door flew open and a small group of its occupants spilled out with guns in hand.

ROGER SEGREST WAS about to scream. He felt it welling up inside him, tried to swallow it, but didn't know if he could keep it down. He flashed back to the night terrors of childhood, when he'd awoken shrieking from horrific dreams, drenched in sweat, his sheets soiled, and the sudden light, his father looming over him, wanting to know exactly what was wrong with his defective son.

This was a lot like that—but ten times worse.

The difference tonight: he wasn't sleeping, his old man was ten years in the grave, and people out there in the dark were real and absolutely trying to kill Segrest.

He took a lull in firing as a signal to escape. And why not, in the circumstances? First, the strangers sent to "save" him from his kidnappers had driven Segrest and the others smack into a firefight, putting them at even greater risk. The one in charge had barked orders at Segrest, as if unaware of his importance back in Washington, clearly forgetting how the pecking order worked, and now the other one was up front, laughing like a lunatic.

Segrest had never been a soldier, but he knew when he was stuck with crazy people.

Time to go.

Without a word to Walton or the others, Segrest rose and scuttled to the APC's back door. The latch was simple, nothing to it. He was reaching for the handle when a firm grip on his shoulder hauled him backward, and he spun around to find the little Arab glaring at him, almost nose to nose.

"You stay inside," the smaller man said.

"Piss off!" Segrest retorted, shoving him away. "You're not the goddamn boss of—"

Suddenly, the man's chest exploded. Blood spattered Segrest's face, and chips of bone or something peppered him like bird shot. He was stumbling backward, retching, when he heard the drumming of machine-gun fire again and realized the lull was over, that he'd missed his chance.

He dropped before the bullets had a chance to cut him down, landed in warm blood. Inches from his face, the Arab's last expression silently rebuked him; no way could Segrest get the last word in this time.

He couldn't argue with a corpse.

The man had died trying to help him, Segrest realized, and he had failed.

No point in screaming now.

BOLAN HAD A choice to make. He could reload the NSV once more and take the charging soldiers down that way, or he could leave the turret and go out to face them with his AKMS carbine. Staying with the APC was safer, at a glance, but if they carried hand grenades, it might turn out to be a grave mistake.

As it turned out, the enemy made Bolan's mind up for him.

One man had stayed behind, still fit to wield the bullet-riddled BTR-152's machine gun. As the others rushed toward Bolan's vehicle, the gunner opened fire, putting his first burst through the shutters masking Bolan's windshield. Bolan felt one of the 12.7 mm slugs pluck at his trouser leg before it traveled on into the troop compartment, seeking other prey.

Before the gunner over there could fire again, Bolan dropped and found another ammo box, sprang up again and started to reload his NSV. The headlights, still glaring out across the desert, let him see the hostile shooter grappling with his own weapon. Reloading? Or had something jammed the other gun?

Whatever it was, Bolan took advantage of the moment, finished feeding his machine gun, locked it down and crouched behind the sights, trying to make his first rounds from the new belt count. The NSV's powerful recoil shuddered through his arms and into Bolan's chest, like a fantastically accelerated heartbeat. Muzzle-flashes hid his human target for an instant, then he saw his tracers striking home, tearing the man on the receiving end apart. The jerky, reeling figure was illuminated by his own light now, his shirt in flames, before he toppled out of sight.

And then the infantry was after him, Kalashnikovs unloading as they came, their bullets pinging off the armor that protected Bolan from their smaller caliber. He cranked the NSV around to greet them, holding down the trigger, giving everything he had to the contenders.

Five men on the ground, all desperate to kill him, but they'd jumped into the wrong game with the wrong opponent. The Executioner's heavy slugs cut through them like a cleaver hacking prime filet, slamming the life out of their bodies as it broke them down into component parts.

He'd have to check the other APC for stragglers playing dead, but Bolan thought the fight was over. He descended from the turret, looking for Sabah Azmeh, then beheld the scene within the troop compartment: Azmeh down and out, the dazed survivors blinking at him like four moles hauled into noonday sun against their will.

"Stay put," he told them in a tone that tolerated no refusal. "I'll be back." Bolan was sorry his guide had not survived the battle. Azmeh was a good man, and Bolan had wanted better for him. But he couldn't dwell on that right now.

Crossing to the other armored vehicle, he peered inside and found no one who seemed to be alive.

Any survivors in the grisly mess would certainly be wounded, likely dying by the pint as blood pulsed out of them, and their vehicle wasn't moving from that spot under its own power, much less resuming a pursuit.

The next step was to check his own ride. He'd already heard the engine rumbling, sounding steady. It had been a lucky break, the opposition gunners trying to kill Bolan, rather than disabling his transport. A walk around showed him five out of six tires still intact, the sixth apparently deflated by a ricochet.

Five tires should be enough, he calculated—if they still had time to make the pickup from Iraq.

His watch said yes, and Bolan trusted it as he climbed back into the driver's seat.

"We're getting tight on time," Ward Simmons said over the Puma's rotor noise.

"I know," Jeff Baxter answered. "One more pass, and this'll go down as a no-show."

"Shame," Craig Rowe chimed in, behind them. "I was lookin' forward to some action."

"That's the last damn thing we need," Baxter reminded him. I'm never working with this flake again, he thought, as if it was his decision.

He started the last pass over the LZ they'd been quoted, eyes sweeping the desert, hoping that he wouldn't see a line of tracers rising up to greet them from the darkness. He had searchlights on the Puma, but he couldn't use them, didn't dare put on a light show for whoever might be prowling over hostile ground nearby.

One final pass, and they could—

"Headlights!" Simmons said, pointing. "One vehicle approaching from the west."

And Baxter saw them now, making a beeline for the pickup site's coordinates. He hovered, making sure he had his radio set for the proper frequency before he spoke into the night.

"To vehicle approaching, this is Backfire Two," he

said, feeling a trifle foolish. "Please, identify. Repeating—"

"This is Striker, Backfire Two," a deep voice answered. "Five to exit."

Only five? "Understood," he told whoever was approaching. "Setting down to meet you now."

And when the link was cut, he turned to Rowe. "Be ready, just in case."

"I'm always ready, man."

They touched down and watched a Russian-manufactured APC roll up, stopping outside the radius of their rotor blades. Five men got out, a soldier leading them in battle dress, the others clad in suits—or parts of suits that had seen better days. Rowe started helping them aboard while Baxter eyed the guy in charge.

"We were expecting eight," he said.

"Two didn't make it out," the soldier said, setting his rifle down. "Wait one for number six."

The big guy ran back to his APC and ducked inside, emerging seconds later with a limp and blood-drenched form over his shoulder in a fireman's carry. Jogging back, he passed his lifeless burden off to Rowe, then dropped into a seat and said, "Okay, we're good to go."

Rowe took him at his word. They lifted off and headed east, toward the sunrise, though it wouldn't lighten the horizon for a few more hours yet. Baxter considered saying something—maybe just to welcome them aboard or put a little levity into the situation— "Hey, rough night?"—but then he caught the solemn soldier watching him and figured he was better off keeping his mouth shut.

Baxter didn't know these people, and he didn't want to know them.

First rule of the game: attend to business and go home alive when you were done.

Tonight, eight of them had achieved that goal. As for the rest, he wished them peace.

Epilogue

Baghdad International Airport

"We're on the same flight," someone said beside Segrest. He'd been halfheartedly browsing the magazines at the newsstand, and now he turned to see his tall, tanned savior in civilian clothes, a carry-on in his hand.

He felt embarrassed, suddenly. "Listen, I know I didn't get around to thanking you."

"Forget it," said the man whose name he didn't know. "All in a day's work."

"Right, for you. It's still my life, though."

"And you're welcome to it."

What did *that* mean? Was he getting a "you're welcome" before saying thanks, or was it some kind of a put-down?

"Anyway, I owe you," Segrest said, forging ahead. "So if there's ever anything you need, something that I can do for you..."

He trailed off. That's if I'm still employed, he thought.

"Just work the cover story," Cooper answered. "You can thank me by forgetting I was ever here."

"Sure thing. About your partner—"

But he was talking to himself. The soldier turned and left, crossing the concourse to an isolated seat behind a pillar, next to a falafel booth.

Some people, Segrest thought, shaking his head. Who knows what makes them tick?

* * * * *

COMING SOON FROM

GOLD EAGLE®

Available October 6, 2015

GOLD EAGLE EXECUTIONER®
UNCUT TERROR – *Don Pendleton*

Mack Bolan sets out to even the score when a legendary Kremlin assassin slaughters an American defector before he can be repatriated. His first target leads him to discover a Russian scheme to crash the Western economy and kill hundreds of innocent people. Only one man can stop it—the Executioner.

GOLD EAGLE STONY MAN®
DEATH MINUS ZERO – *Don Pendleton*

Washington goes on full alert when Chinese operatives kidnap the creator of a vital US defense system. While Phoenix Force tracks the missing scientist, Able Team uncovers a plot to take over the system's mission control. Now both teams must stop America's enemies from holding the country hostage.

GOLD EAGLE SUPERBOLAN™
DEAD RECKONING – *Don Pendleton*

A US consulate is bombed, its staff mercilessly killed. The terrorists scatter to hideouts around the globe, but Mack Bolan hunts them down three by three. When the last one vanishes, the world's leaders are caught in the crosshairs and the Executioner must stop the terrorists' global deathblow.

Bolan began to run with a renewed sense of urgency. Suddenly, off to his left he saw something that looked like a life preserver on a stormy sea: metal rungs in the side of the concrete wall, forming a ladder leading to the street.

"Jack," Bolan called. "Look."

Grimaldi fired off two more rounds and glanced over his right shoulder. His grin seemed to get larger.

Bolan got to the ladder and pulled on the first rung, testing its sturdiness. He backed into the wall, taking some of Framer's weight off his legs. Grimaldi was at his side now. Bolan noticed the Beretta's slide was locked back. He grabbed the weapon, dropped the magazine and inserted a new one. Turning his head slightly he addressed Framer.

"Our only chance is to get up this ladder to the street. Think you can make it?"

He shook his head. "Leave me here. I'm too weak."

The man's face was grayish. They had to get him medical attention soon, very soon. Bolan motioned for Grimaldi to go up first.

"I'll bring him up while you do cover fire," Bolan said. "Be ready to help me lift him when we get near the top."

Without another word Grimaldi quickly began scaling the iron rungs.

Bolan saw movement about fifty yards away, then a pinpoint muzzle flash. Wherever the round went, it didn't seem to be close to them. Rather than return useless fire, he waited.

Seconds later Grimaldi called down to him: "Clear up here so far."

Holstering the Beretta, the Executioner turned back to Framer. "Listen," Bolan said. "I'm going to climb up the ladder. You've got to hold on to me with all you've got. Ready?"

Framer grunted a yes.

Bolan waited for the man to secure his grip, then began climbing. The extra weight made every movement difficult, but the soldier continued the rigorous ascent.

When they were halfway up, Bolan tried to count the number of rungs to the top. Perhaps fifteen more. Fifteen, fourteen, thirteen?

The iron rung under his left hand popped loose from its concrete socket.

Framer screamed.

Bolan tightened his grip on the other rung, avoiding the deadly plunge.

Lucky thirteen, he thought, readjusting his grip and reaching for the next rung.

Don't miss
UNCUT TERROR by Don Pendleton,
available October 2015 wherever
Gold Eagle® books and ebooks are sold.

DON PENDLETON'S *MACK BOLAN*®

"Sanctioned by the Oval Office, Mack Bolan's mandate is to defuse threats against Americans and to protect the innocent and powerless anywhere in the world."

This longer format series features Mack Bolan and presents action/adventure storylines with an epic sweep that includes subplots. Bolan is supported by the Stony Man Farm teams, and can elicit assistance from allies that he encounters while on mission.

Available wherever Gold Eagle® books and ebooks are sold.

GOLD EAGLE®

GESB2015